MW01415477

[m]otherhood

[m]otherhood

anna lea JANCEWICZ

[m]otherhood
Copyright © 2018 by Anna Lea Jancewicz

Published by Widow & Orphan House, LLC
widowandorphanhouse.com

All rights reserved. No part of this book may be reproduced in any manner whatsoever without written permission of the author *and* publisher except in the case of brief quotations embodied in critical articles and reviews. For information, contact: editor@widowandorphanhouse.com

FIRST EDITION

ISBN: 978-0-9984037-6-2
Library of Congress Control Number: 2018900326

Cover image a detail from "Mutter und Kind" by Egon Schiele (PD-US)

Book design by Matt Warren and Amy Warren
Jacket design by Matt Warren and Amy Warren

Set in Spectrum MT Std
Published and printed in the United States of America

Thank you to the magazines in which the following stories first appeared, some in slightly different versions:

Phantom Drift: "Vaginal Disturbances"
Wyvern Lit: "Chana Finkelstein Made a Golem Baby"
Far Enough East: "Valerie and the Rat"
Cease, Cows: "The Water"
Third Point Press: "Funny How Tender Can Mean Two Things"
Witch Craft Magazine: "Rosemary & Ghostmilk"
Syntax & Salt: "The Shearing of Yossi Mandelbaum"
FRiGG: "The Womanly Art of Drag Racing"
Scrutiny: "Bird Was Gone"
Bartleby Snopes: "Sheitel"
Atticus Review: "Off the Map"

THANK YOU Claudia Mazur for telling me to write again. Thank you to the women of the Norfolk Writers Workshop: Lydia Netzer, Ellen Bryson, Antonia Giordano, and Alicia Dekker. Without you this book would not exist. Thanks to the Muse Writers Center, to Eric Ramseier and all my fellow writers in his workshop. Thank you to the online community of writers and editors who have given me much support, especially Katie Mead-Brewer, Georgia Bellas, Asha Doré, Kathy Fish, Ani King, and Alina Stefanescu. Thank you Ellen Parker, your editing of "The Womanly Art of Drag Racing" was brilliant and awed me. Thank you to my beta readers Vanessa Wagner, April Mathis, Chance Puma, Jennifer Gibson, and Stacia Sanders. Thank you to my husband David for making me a room of my own, and for saying all the funny and fucked up things that make their way into my dialogue. Thank you to my grrrl and my mancub. Thank you to everybody at the Van Wyck Branch of the Norfolk Public Library. Thank you to the ghost of Shirley Jackson.

"No live organism can continue for long to exist sanely under conditions of absolute reality; even larks and katydids are supposed, by some, to dream."

—Shirley Jackson, *The Haunting of Hill House*

Contents

Killing Anthony Wasn't Good Enough   *1*
Vaginal Disturbances   *13*
Chana Finkelstein Made a Golem Baby   *35*
Valerie and the Rat   *45*
The Water   *53*
Funny How Tender Can Mean Two Things   *57*
Rosemary & Ghostmilk   *67*
The Shearing of Yossi Mandelbaum   *71*
The Womanly Art of Drag Racing   *83*
Bird Was Gone   *101*
The Female of the Species   *109*
Mama Loves the Baby and the Baby Loves the Mama   *123*
Sheitel   *151*
Off the Map   *159*

[m]otherhood

Killing anthony wasn't good enough

There was an awful lot of blood to clean up after Sylvia murdered her husband. She'd expected that, of course, and had planned accordingly, buying the yellow latex dish gloves and a new scrub brush for the occasion. She'd even splurged on the name-brand paper towels that promised super absorbency. Anthony would have given her an earful over that purchase, for sure. He would have told her that making do with more affordable paper towels just meant she had to use a little elbow grease and stop being so lazy. But now Anthony's skull was crushed, so his opinions about Sylvia's housekeeping skills didn't really matter so much. And whatever was to come, she'd never again have to go through the grocery receipts with him line by line, justifying the expense of each item. Sylvia was very pleased by that thought.

She got down on her hands and knees and began to scrub the kitchen floor. The smell of bleach stung her nostrils. The knees of her overalls would be destroyed, but that was okay. Sacrifices had to be made. Life was like that. The radio was playing Red Hot

Chili Peppers and that was a good groove for cleaning. Sylvia said out loud *That is so true. There's just no stopping spirits when they need you.*

The kids were going to the sitter's house after school, so she had plenty of time to get the job done. Sylvia had packed extra snacks for them in their insulated lunch bags. Carrot sticks, hummus, little shelf-stable boxes of organic chocolate milk with smiling cartoon cows. Sylvia cared deeply about her children's nutrition.

Anthony was crammed into the shower stall in the downstairs bathroom, swaddled in a pink shower curtain liner. Transporting his body from the kitchen hadn't been as difficult as Sylvia imagined it would be. Anthony wasn't that bulky. Truth be told, she'd often wondered how in the world she'd ended up married to a man who was only taller than she was by a few inches. After the third baby, Sylvia had outweighed him by fifty pounds. Now, she definitely saw the advantage of his slight stature. His easy portability was a nice surprise.

He'd always gotten really upset about being called short, and insisted that he was *medium height*. Sylvia smiled at the memory. She scrubbed vigorously at a particularly stubborn patch of gore on the linoleum and said aloud *Fuck you, Napoleon.*

When Sylvia first began planning the murder, she'd thought about poison. She'd considered shooting him, too. But when it came down to it, when she really searched her feelings, what she truly wanted was to beat Anthony to death with a baseball bat. So that's what she did. She stood in the kitchen waiting for him to come home from work, holding an aluminum baseball bat. He slammed the front door behind him as he always did, and tromped across the living room carpet in his dirty work boots. Sylvia was forever asking him to take off his shoes at the door, but Anthony always refused. *Keeping the floor clean is your job, not mine. Do I ask you to come to the shop and weld shit for me? No, I do not.* Sylvia heard him dump his stuff on the dining room table. She knew he'd be coming straight for the refrigerator. Anthony thought he was going to pop open his first can of after-work beer, just like any other day. But that was not going to happen.

The thing was, she'd known he'd be armed. He always was, since he'd acquired his cherished concealed carry permit. She'd known he'd have his Smith & Wesson M&P Shield 9mm securely holstered at the small of his back. As if he really needed that for his work commute. He even wore the damn thing when he was out in the yard raking leaves. He was such an asshole.

So, Sylvia did not have a margin of error. If he had a moment to figure out what was going down, she could conceivably be in serious danger. There had to be no hesitation, no dicking around like a supervillain, announcing her intentions and enumerating her grievances. She felt kind of disappointed about that, actually. She'd planned on maybe getting talky if there was an opportunity after he was really fucked up but not quite dead. It didn't pan out though. Once she was in the zone, she couldn't stop.

Sylvia hit him hard and fast as he rounded the corner to the kitchen. The bat collided with his head and there was a very satisfying crack. He hit the floor, throwing his arms up to defend his face. Sylvia kept swinging. It was really pretty simple. She was glad she hadn't gone with a more complicated plan.

Post-murder was the bitch.

Sylvia wasn't really a fan of those procedural cop shows, so it wasn't like she had a bunch of useful information on hand about cleaning up evidence. She'd tried to watch some in preparation, but they really either grossed her out or bored her to tears. She figured she shouldn't Google things either, because that could come back to bite her in the ass later. She just tried to be smart about it, best she could. She scrubbed the kitchen down several times. After she hacked Anthony to pieces in the shower stall and packaged him up neatly, she cleaned the bathroom like nobody's business too.

It was winter and getting dark pretty early, so she waited until it was reasonably dim before carrying the bags out to the car. She hid the pieces of Anthony at the bottom of paper grocery sacks, with various outgrown children's clothes and busted toys on top. Sure enough, her neighbor Christina caught her in the act.

Taking another load to the thrift store? she asked as she dropped a bulging Hefty bag into the green city trashcans stationed between their houses.

Yep Sylvia said, smiling. *Almost the end of the year. You know Anthony wants to get that tax deduction.*

Christina nodded and Sylvia slammed the hatchback shut.

She drove to six different dumpsters around town. Anthony's remains were securely packaged in freezer paper like meat, marked with false expiration dates and then wound in an enormous quantity of plastic wrap. His smashed phone and his gun disappeared into the dirty gray water of the river. She stopped off at the thrift store last, to actually donate the other items from the bags. She folded the receipt neatly and slipped it into her purse. Then she headed toward the babysitter's place. She hoped that the kids had finished all their homework and not wasted their afternoon playing Minecraft.

For dinner, Sylvia made a new recipe she'd been wanting to try. *Chicken Curry in a Hurry.* She substituted brown rice for white, of course. The children asked for seconds, so she counted it as a success. She complained that Anthony had not made it home yet. She tried calling him three times. Sylvia thought that seemed like a reasonable amount of concern. She told the boys they could watch just two episodes of *Adventure Time* before bed, and told Dana to fetch the brush and detangle spray so they could commence with the nightly ordeal of grooming her hair. Dana's hair almost reached her waist now, thick brown curls that were always snarled into a mass at the back of her head by the end of the day. Dana cried every night as Sylvia dragged the brush through her hair.

Wait Sylvia said as Dana started for the bathroom. *Get the scissors from under the bathroom sink too.*

Dana stared at her mother in disbelief. *But Daddy says I can't cut my hair.*

It was true. Anthony had told the girl *Your mother only wants to cut your hair because she's jealous of you.*

Well, Daddy's not here now.

Sylvia snipped at Dana's hair until it was a cute, manageable bob. Dana liked it. She smiled at herself in the mirror, and ran right away to call her bestie Amanda. Sylvia washed up the dinner dishes.

After the kids were all tucked into bed, Sylvia sat at the kitchen table and reviewed her plans for the next day. She would call Anthony's work looking for him. She would call his friends. Then hospitals. Eventually, she would make a panicked call to the police. She was very glad that Anthony took the bus to work, so she needn't worry about the car. That would have made things more difficult. There was the chance that one of the neighbors had seen him walking home from the bus stop yesterday, but shit, she couldn't control everything. Sylvia brewed a pot of coffee and started in on another round of cleaning the kitchen and downstairs bath. This time, she listened to the Pixies. Anthony always hated the Pixies. What kind of dickhead hates the Pixies? Sylvia said out loud *Can you imagine that? A coy koi.* An image bubbled up from the bottom of her brain, a half-forgotten classic cartoon fish blinking its swollen purple eyelids seductively. Sylvia imagined

Anthony's ugly mug on the fish and giggled. Startled, the fish swished its filmy femme fins and vanished.

It was really late when she finished, but Sylvia decided to take her time in a hot bath anyway. In the upstairs bathroom. Her arms and legs ached. She was wiped out. Murder should definitely count as cardio. She added Epsom salts under the tap and slipped into the steaming water. She rubbed the unmelted crystals under her hands, swishing them along the bottom of the tub. Then she lay back and soaked in peace for a good half hour. She really didn't think about anything at all. She made a few little moans of pleasure.

Sylvia figured it was too late to bother with taking her melatonin supplement. She'd be too drowsy in the morning and she needed her wits about her. She probably wouldn't need it to sleep anyway. Who was going to keep her awake with their snoring? She laughed.

Anthony, the fucker. Sylvia's eyes sprang open. The red numbers of the digital alarm clock showed it was 3:58. Anthony was snoring, loud and hard. She turned and reached out her arm to swat at him, but her hand fell flat to the mattress.

Oh, shit.

She remembered.

Sylvia bolted upright, scanning the room. Sweat beaded her forehead.

What kind of fucked-up Telltale Heart bullshit is this?!

There was no answer. Only snoring.

Sylvia grabbed everything off the nightstand. Books, water glass, Anthony's stupid grippy hand exercise thing. She flung each object into the dark, screaming.

Fuck you! Shut the fuck up!

But the snoring didn't stop.

Sylvia scooped up her feather pillow and grabbed the blanket. It trailed behind her down the hall, down the stairs, to the couch. She'd done this a thousand times before. She threw herself down on the couch and pulled the blanket over her head.

You bastard she said.

During the days that followed, everything was cool. Remarkably cool. Sure, Sylvia was questioned. Were they fighting? No, they were not. (She'd been so good at taking his shit.) Was there another woman? Not that she knew of, she never suspected so. (Who the hell would want him?) Did Anthony have a life insurance policy? No, he did not. (Fucker.) The house was given a cursory search. The police really didn't suspect foul play. He was missing, but not presumed dead. The detective on the case had it in his head that Anthony was a deadbeat, that he'd skipped out on her. Didn't want to deal with a divorce, didn't want to pay child support. That was very convenient. Sylvia didn't know for sure what Anthony's co-workers had said about him, she didn't get the details, but the detective hinted that they'd had plenty to say and that they'd mentioned he complained a lot about money. The theory took root and blossomed in the gossip of the PTA moms. They looked at Sylvia with false pity, sizing her up and guessing at what she'd done to run Anthony off. The ladies at the church took up a collection to help the family get by. Sylvia trotted off to Wegman's straight away and bought chicken breasts instead of thighs, and good toilet paper. The children were wiping their asses with cushiony soft Charmin for the first time in their lives.

So, yes, the days that followed had Sylvia breathing a sigh of relief. The days. But at night, she was ready to start ripping her hair out at the roots. The snoring did not cease. She was absolutely sure that she was not losing her mind. For one thing, it wasn't like she was racked with guilt. It certainly wasn't going to be the kind of thing where regret drove her to madness and confession. Screw that. Poe could suck it.

The snoring was not inside her head, not like that. It was obvious that the kids didn't hear it, but it wasn't just sawing away between her ears all the time. It was only nocturnal, and its locus was the bedroom. Sylvia could flee to the couch to lessen her misery, or at least to turn down the volume. She could still hear it faintly from downstairs, just as she could when Anthony was alive. She was not nuts. Anthony was haunting her. Even from beyond the grave, Anthony was still being an asshole.

Sylvia thought about switching bedrooms with the boys, but from their room the noise was much more annoying than it was from the couch, so that would be useless. She thought about buying a more comfortable couch, but that just pissed her off. It would mean surrender. She had to figure out a way to *win*. Obviously, killing Anthony wasn't good enough.

She took her melatonin. She drank valerian root tea. She used ear plugs.

One Thursday evening, as she was ladling out crockpot chicken enchiladas for the boys before their wrestling meet, she had the bright spark of a better idea. As much as it pained Sylvia to admit it, she'd come to realize that balls-to-the-wall revenge wasn't always the most effective tack. Sometimes, even the most hardcore bitch could catch more flies with crockpot enchiladas than with a baseball bat. Anthony had really loved her enchiladas. She was thinking it might be possible to lure Anthony's ghost into a trap by using his favorite foods.

And, of course, shitty beer.

Sylvia sent the children to her mother's house for the weekend. She packed their backpacks with fresh underwear and flannel pajamas and healthy snacks. She made sure they all had library books picked out to bring along. She put them on the train and stopped off for groceries on the way home. Snow was expected. It was going to be a cozy housebound weekend whether or not she succeeded in raising her murdered husband from the dead with garbage snacks and PBR. She got herself an extra box of wine.

Sylvia planned on making more enchiladas, but she also filled her cart with all the other regular gross shit Anthony liked. Cans of creamed corn. Garishly colored popsicles in plastic tubes. Sardines in mustard sauce. Wonder Bread, to be smeared with mayonnaise and sugar. Chocolate pudding cups. Slim Jims. Christ, his gut had been a dumpster.

She started drinking from her box of wine as soon as she got the enchiladas into the crockpot. By the time the afternoon had grown dark, the snow coming down heavily, Sylvia was more than half lit. She scooped out a mess of gooey Mexican onto a plate, and arranged it on a tray with all the rest of the food. She balanced the tray in one hand and held the six-pack of beer in the other. She climbed the stairs carefully. It wasn't that easy to do. Sylvia wobbled.

She set up the tray on the bed. She steeled herself for what was coming next. She'd decided to put on the godawful Walmart lingerie that Anthony had bought for her last Christmas. She'd worn it for him just the once, because he kept bitching about it, but he had passed out before things progressed any further than Sylvia twirling sullenly on the bedroom carpet. It was a one-piece monstrosity, slippery and red, with scratchy lace and an underwire that jammed into her armpits. Made in China. Probably by a six-year-old. Worst of all, he'd bought it a size too small. She supposed she should be thankful he'd underestimated her figure instead of overestimating. She squeezed into it now and stood there nauseated, feeling like a reject from *Rocky Horror*.

Annnnnthony she called. *C'mon baby. C'mon out and play.*

There was a glimmer of something weird in the air, near the closet.

Ennnnnchiladas Sylvia cooed.

Nothing more happened. She was getting impatient. Then she had an idea. She picked up a can of beer and snapped open the top.

Goddamn if that didn't work instantly. It was like his natural mating call or something. She could see a vague outline of his body, all static and fuzz, pop into being. His greasy little mustache was the first part to solidify, wouldn't you know it.

Anthony's ghost didn't look fucked up at all. Sylvia had been worried that he'd appear gruesome, with evidence of the head-bashing he'd taken, or even worse, chopped into bits, just a heap of meat and bones, as he was when she last stared down at him, dismembered in the shower stall. But Anthony looked perfectly normal, which was to say he was scowling. His protruding brow was furrowed tightly and he was sucking his teeth.

You bitch he said. *You really killed the fuck outta me.*

But I've got popsicles Sylvia said. She jutted her hip and tilted her head. *And I wore this for you.*

I can't believe you beat me to death with a baseball bat.

Yeah, I did. But there's beers.

This was the trick part. Sylvia had already emptied out one of the cans, pouring the beer down the drain of the kitchen sink. She held that empty can out toward Anthony. She could see it in his eyes that he didn't quite trust her. The murder had really clued him in to her true feelings. He squinted a little. He breathed heavily through his nose. Sylvia jiggled the can in her grip and whispered *Beeeeeer.* He reached for it on instinct. He couldn't help himself, the dumb fuck. Sylvia pounced.

She grabbed him by the wrist, and his arm collapsed into a bright slimy mess. She held on tight. Anthony struggled. He wriggled and bucked. He cursed and sputtered. *Bitch! Bitch!*

By the time Sylvia got all of Anthony's ghost crammed into the empty PBR can, her Walmart lingerie was covered in ectoplasm. That stuff stunk to high hell. One of the shiny red spaghetti straps had snapped, and her left boob hung out. Her hair was wild, and crusty with drying slime. She stoppered the can with a generous slathering of Bondo and wrapped it in a whole roll of duct tape. It was surprisingly light, really. She sat cross-legged on the bedroom carpet, cradling it in one sticky palm.

Her first thought had been to bury the can in the backyard, but the ground was frozen and that seemed like it would be way too much work. Maybe impossible. She had already put so much effort into this murder, and she really wanted to take a nice hot shower and catch up on a little television. She could put on her fluffy bathrobe and watch *Orange is the New Black* right out in the open on the living room TV while the kids were out of the house. Sylvia considered bricking the can up in the basement, Cask of Amontillado-style. But that was pretty time-consuming too. The poetry of it really wouldn't be worth it. She could squirrel it away in a box in the attic, but if they had another raccoon invasion up there, Anthony's ghost might get inadvertently freed. Those raccoons had made a real mess of her scrapbooking totes that last time.

It occurred to Sylvia that it might be smart to keep it someplace pretty accessible, someplace where she could check up on it.

Someplace where she'd have a chance to take it out every once in a while and savor her victory.

Maa awm Dana whined, breaking the word into two long syllables, the universally understood indicator of adolescent impatience. *Are you done in there yet? We're all just waiting on you.*

A few more minutes, please!

It was a beautiful spring Sunday. Sylvia had woken bright and early, feeling very well rested. The picnic basket was packed.

Sylvia had made adorable little no-crust sandwiches, inspired by a Pinterest idea, substituting whole grain bread for the white. She'd carved raw vegetables into charming shapes, and wrapped up individual packets of jellybeans for each of the children for surprise treats. They were quality jelly beans, made from real fruit, sweetened with organic honey, without a trace of artificial dyes or preservatives. They were still candy, yes, but Sylvia felt that on occasion, a mother just needed to do something a little wild and unexpected to make everybody happy. Sylvia cared deeply about her family's happiness.

She stepped out of the shower onto the bathmat and toweled herself dry. She rubbed herself down with coconut oil, flossed her teeth, swabbed her ears. She pulled on her bathrobe and proceeded to blow out her hair. When she flipped her head up and caught sight of herself in the mirrored door of the medicine cabinet, she smiled. She wrapped up the hairdryer in its cord, and returned it to its place under the sink. She reached for the light switch, but then paused. One last little thing.

Sylvia lifted the heavy porcelain lid from the toilet tank and peered down into the cold still water.

Safe and sound, baby she said. *Safe and sound.*

Vaginal Disturbances

At 11:53 on a Thursday afternoon in March, after a lively morning of scrubbing congealed dog vomit from the kitchen floor, incinerating two consecutive batches of banana pancakes, powering through a potty-training fiasco of epic magnitude, and listening to her four-year-old daughter's earnest yet harrowing rendition of *Let It Go* at least a dozen times, Rita lost her shit while struggling impotently to fold a fitted sheet, and locked herself in the upstairs bathroom. She sat down on the fluffy pink toilet seat cover with her head in her hands, and began to cry.

Fat little toddler fingers appeared under the door, wriggling moistly against the ceramic tile, threatening to snatch away Rita's small measure of solitude. *Ma-maaa!* her son wailed. The thud of his head against the cheap glue-board panel of the door echoed in the tiny bathroom, establishing a savage rhythm that Rita imagined was not unlike the pounding war drums of some brute cannibal tribe. *Boo-beees! Mine! Now!* he shrieked. *Ah* Rita muttered. *It's true, the little barbarian wants to eat me alive.*

She stood, her thighs rubbery, and smoothed the ruffles of her vintage apron, one of many in the collection that had been swelling to dangerous proportions as she alternately battled against and succumbed to her Etsy addiction. Rita looked at herself in the toothpaste-freckled mirror, squinting to blur the enlarged pores and deepening furrows that she'd recently discovered, much to her shock, after replacing her six-year-old eyeglass prescription. She was turning forty in a few months. She hadn't had a good night's sleep since Jacob had been born. She was pretty sure she was having a hot flash right that minute. The backs of her knees were sweating.

Before she could reach for the locked knob in defeat, her daughter Abigail joined in the hallway insurgency, running full speed and aiming a flying karate kick at the door as she loosed a guttural *Hi-ya!* Rita startled, her eyes bolting to the undersize bathroom window. For a split second, she genuinely considered her chances with the narrow squeeze and the two-story drop. She couldn't breathe. She could feel her veins constricting, and there were sparkles in her periphery. An elephant pirouetting on her chest. She gripped the rim of the sink with one blanched and trembling hand. And then, just as she surrendered to the inevitability of losing consciousness, she was overcome by the mightiest, most deeply satisfying sneeze of her life.

It was at that moment that she felt the first lost object emerge from her vagina.

It was a bizarre sensation, a dislodging of something deep within her, from a numinous place of which she had been completely unaware. She reached into her sturdy granny-panties with trepidation, and removed the mystery item. It was a lead gaming miniature. Without a doubt, Rita had hand-painted the figure herself, with great care, at her boyfriend Rob's kitchen table, at the age of fifteen. Rita had, somehow, expelled Zoltana of the Borderlands, thirty-third level Magic-User, badass champion of hundreds of D&D campaigns, from her cunt.

After the second baby was born, Rita discovered that she had a tampon problem. Her cycle resumed when Jacob was thirteen months old, on a blustery late autumn morning when it was not yet light and she was enjoying a rare quiet moment while everybody else slept soundly. Their soft snoring bloated the bedroom while the shadows of wind-whipped trees scudded across its walls. She'd awoke with a dull cramping, and soon felt the warm wet release of blood. *Fuck* she said, scurrying out from under the feather blanket and down the hall to the toilet.

She knelt on the floor to rummage under the bathroom sink. She was sure that there had to be a tampon stashed somewhere in the jumble of hygienic items crammed behind the fire extinguisher and the basket of cheerful plastic tub toys. She found one lonely o.b. tucked inside the make-up bag she hadn't unzipped in at least a year. It would do. Rita inserted the cotton plug with an exhalation of resignation, and decided she'd best get started on breakfast before the baby woke up. She would need to pack up the kids and head out to the drugstore as soon as they'd destroyed their oatmeal and scrambled eggs.

But when she returned home later that morning clutching her mega-size box of store-brand Tampax knock-offs with cardboard applicators, she had made an unwitting mistake. It didn't take her long to figure out that her vagina would no longer accept these standard-length stoppers. They didn't fit properly. They were uncomfortable. It felt as if they were sliding out, as if something was *pushing* them out. Rita immediately suspected that her vagina was harboring a tumor that would, no doubt, cause her untimely death and leave her children to practically fend for themselves as her husband flailed helplessly. He would feed them sporadic and unwholesome microwaved dinners. They would whimper dolefully, in ill-fitting shoes, as he improperly loaded the dishwasher.

That night, Rita asked her husband if anything felt *different* in there. He paused, mid-stroke, to consider, shifting his hips as if to gauge any discrepancy with his instrument.

Nope he said. *Feels good. Feels warm and wet and good.*

He nuzzled her neck, resumed his thrust.

Because I think I might have a tumor she said. *I'm having trouble with my tampons.*

Yeah said her husband, with an exaggerated moan. *Talk to me about menstrual products. That is so hot.*

Rita spent the next two days anxiously ruminating on the tumor, steeling herself for the worst, growing teary-eyed while gazing at the truly beautiful faces of her poor babies who would probably not even remember her. When she just couldn't stand it any longer, she sat down to Google her surely fatal prognosis.

As it turned out, her tampon problem was just one of those Things Nobody Tells You About Childbirth. Apparently, the planet was just teeming with panicked postpartum mothers unable to effectively grasp the conveniently disposable wads with their woefully collapsed vaginal walls. Mommy message boards across the internet were virtually distended with a glut of women, represented by cute cartoon avatars of themselves, all suffering silently in real life. Emboldened by pseudonyms like *katiesmommy* and *mom2twoboys*, they spilled their guts in insomniac posts for anybody online who would offer words of encouragement. Replies were saturated with encouraging emoticons. There was enthusiastic debate over squats vs. kegels. Some mothers confessed to slogging through their bloody days in cumbersome maxi-pads. Some of them waxed evangelical about moon cups and natural sea-sponges. Most of the women reported that they had been able to use the shorter o.b. tampons.

Rita was stunned. None of her friends had ever mentioned such a thing. It wasn't a topic that came up at Mommy & Me story time, or even at La Leche League meetings, where over-sharing was as pervasive as gluten-free brownies or amber teething necklaces. She was, of course, relieved that the likelihood of her vagina cultivating a monstrous growth had plummeted, but she was also disappointed and appalled that so many of her comadres were mum on the subject. Rita was also just not totally convinced that something else, something weird, wasn't brewing in her uterine realm.

Within a few months, she was certain of it. Rita had always been unshakably regular with her cycle. Seven days of flow. Every 28 days, without fail. Ovulation on day 14. The moon had looked to Rita to set its clock. But not anymore. Sometimes, her cycle was a few days short. Sometimes, on day 14 it just started all over again. And her flow was often scant, lasting only a few days. Or, sometimes she would bleed so heavily that she produced large clots that dangled from her tampon like fat, glistening, carmine fruits that filled her with horror. Rita called her doctor.

With her socked feet in the stirrups, lying supine as her kids scurried in a frenzy over every sanitized surface in the exam room, Rita asked Dr. Bloch how everything looked in there.

Everything looks healthy and normal she replied buoyantly. *Now this might pinch a little.*

All right, because my tampons don't fit anymore and I thought it was probably a tumor but the internet says I'm okay.

Dr. Bloch giggled. She was in her twenties and wore cute dresses. With belts.

Yes, there is some collapse in the vaginal walls. You've had two babies, and that's to be expected.

Rita had also never seen her without five-inch heels. Her vagina was probably tight as a fist.

You'll get the results of your pap within the week she said. *That screens for cervical cancer, not uterine or ovarian cancer. But to be honest, I think what you've told me sounds well within normal for a woman of your age.*

A woman of her age. Rita popped her head up to look at Dr. Bloch. She wanted to counter that with some funny quip, but she was at a loss. And she saw that Jacob was stomping on the pedal to the biohazard trash bin, its lid flapping open and closed, like a highly infectious Muppet mouth.

Jacob, baby, that's gross. Eww. Leave that alone. So what, you're saying I'm in menopause?

No, not menopause. That's after you've ceased menstruation. But perimenopause, the period leading up to it, can span eight to twelve years. Your body will go through changes.

Abigail reached up and grabbed the stethoscope hanging over Dr. Bloch's shoulder, and gripping it like a microphone, began belting out the opening lyrics to *Let It Go*.

Abby, please. That's expensive. And delicate.

Dr. Bloch pried it gently from her hands and promised *When I'm all done with Mommy, you can listen to your brother's heartbeat, okay?*

She turned back to Rita. *Have you been having other symptoms? Insomnia?*

Are you kidding me? Rita asked. *Jacob still wakes up to nurse, like, six times a night.*

I do see you've gained a bit of weight since your last appointment.

Rita reminded herself that *Fuck you* was likely never a proper response during a gyno exam. *Umm-hmm* she nodded.

Well, these things may be related to changing hormone levels. Or, you know, you could also just being going through a time of stress. Do you feel like you have a lot of stress right now?

Jacob snatched a speculum off Dr. Bloch's wheeled tray and pointed it at her face.

Pew! Pew! Pew! Pew! Shoot you!

Stress? asked Rita. She let her head drop back onto the crinkly paper. *Fuck.*

Fuck! repeated Jacob. *Fuck! Fuck! Fuck!*

Rita didn't know what she ought to do with Zoltana of the Borderlands. So she tucked the miniature into the pocket of her apron and lurched out into the hallway in a daze. She was 100% certain that the Mayo Clinic's online guide to perimenopausal symptoms had not included a single cross-reference to the Monster Manual. She'd read it at least half a dozen times, along with every book on the subject in the public library's collection. She'd been following the sage advice of lovely silver-haired authors with stylishly funky, chunky jewelry. Popping flaxseed oil capsules three times a day, taking B-complex vitamin supplements that turned her pee neon yellow, and rubbing dollops of a recommended brand of natural progesterone cream into all the approved sweet spots of the most permeable skin on her body. She'd been applying the cream every morning and night from day 12 to day 26, alternating areas religiously for optimal absorption. She'd been eating more oily fish and taking brisk walks in the neighborhood in the evenings. True, she was still as exhausted as ever, napping in the afternoons every chance she got. She still had less than zero interest in sex, although she hadn't actually revealed that bit of info to her husband. She was still having mood swings, her periods still weren't always regular. She'd figured that these things take time to sort themselves out, but now this. Now this. The Boston Women's Health Collective had some freaking explaining to do. She'd been seeking guidance from gynecologists and expert herbalists, when apparently what she needed was a Dungeon Master.

Rita spread a plastic drop cloth over the dining room table and set out finger paints and Play-dough for the kids while she got started on lunch. She gave Zoltana a perch on the back of the stove, and gazed at the tiny figure as she stirred a boiling pot of corkscrew noodles. Rita was sure she hadn't laid eyes on Zoltana in at least twenty years. All of her RPG stuff had been lost, after she dropped out of art school and hadn't had the cash to retrieve her belongings from the storage unit she'd rented, before she skipped town and headed back home. Zoltana of the Borderlands. The character had been Rita's crowning achievement. Not only a mind-blowing sorceress, but a truly unequaled fighter. Legendary. With a killer rack, of course. As a teenager, Rita had not been overly concerned with feminist body politics.

She drained the pasta in a whoosh of steam, cooled it with water from the tap.

Do you guys want salmon in your noodles, or salami? she called out.

Salmon! Abigail screamed. *I want to be a bear! I want salmon and honey!*

I'm not putting honey in the noodles Rita said. *But salmon I can do, Baby Bear.*

Nooo! Jacob whined. *No samma! Swami! Swami!*

How DARE you?! Abigail interjected. *Bears do NOT like salami!*

Rita heard a distinct *thwap*. And Abigail's sharply ascending wail.

Jacob punched me in my face! In my FACE!

Rita sank down onto the linoleum and sat cross-legged, massaging her own shoulders. Her vagina was rife with some kind of powerful and mysterious witchcraft. She did not know why Zoltana was here, after all these years. But she was sure of one thing. Zoltana of the Borderlands may have defeated orcs, vanquished demons, and extinguished the fires of immortal dragons, but she had never had to put up with this kind of shit.

Luke.

Yeah, say my name her husband said, speeding up his pumping.

Be serious. I have something serious I want to tell you.

This is totally the best time for serious conversation. Go ahead.

He hooked his arm under the back of Rita's left knee and pushed it up to her shoulder.

Well, it's when we have time alone together. Anyway, something kind of, well, actually, something very weird came out of my vagina today.

Do we have to talk about disgusting things right now?

Disgusting things? You mean, like, my vagina? Is that too disgusting to talk about during intercourse?

You promised. You promised you'd stop saying "intercourse."

Right. Sorry. So you think vaginas are disgusting? Are you gay?

I love it when you ask me if I'm gay while we're doing it.

You mean during intercourse? With my vagina?

Your vagina, the one that something "weird" came out of?

Seriously, it was really weird.

I have something weird for your vagina.

Oh, Christ. Can you just hurry up and finish?

Mmm. Yeah, I love it when you say that.

Two weeks passed with Zoltana tucked inside Rita's apron pocket as she cut the crusts off peanut butter sandwiches, supervised egg-carton art projects, offered bribes of M&M's for turds deposited neatly in the happy frog potty instead of on the hallway carpet. She read aloud the same soul-deadening board book rhymes ad nauseam. She completed eighteen loads of laundry, stepped on Legos five times, and managed to take six and a half showers. One of them was interrupted by a life-or-death cracked juice box straw emergency before she could actually wash her hair.

Rita hadn't tried to talk to her husband again about her vaginal disturbance. She decided against bringing the matter to Dr. Bloch's attention, as she wasn't feeling up to a psych referral. She'd almost convinced herself that the incident had been, in fact, a hallucination precipitated by panic attack. Almost. Because any time she pleased, she could reach her hand into her apron pocket and look right at evidence to the contrary.

Rita hadn't planned on carrying Zoltana with her to the supermarket that Monday afternoon near the end of March. It just kind of happened. After having to literally wrestle Jacob into a pair of pants, and pin him down on the floor with her heels on his shoulders to get shoes on his feet, Rita had collapsed face-down on the living room carpet to take a few deep breaths. The miniature, tucked into her apron pocket as usual, had been stabbing her in the hip bone, and Rita had slipped it into the back pocket of her jeans as Abigail ran in circles around her depleted form, singing an impromptu song about grocery shopping. Abigail loved going grocery shopping, as her lyrics reminded Rita. There was no errand Rita hated doing more with the kids along for the ride. She always put it off until the pantry was bare. She would try to convince her husband that grocery shopping was a task that she should accomplish solo, in the evening, when he was available to watch the kids, and he would say something sweet and supportive, like *Not my problem, dude. Suck it up. I have shit to do tonight.* The only thing worse than taking her kids to the supermarket was having to deal with Derek at the check-out.

Derek. Even just thinking his name was like biting into a wad of gristle. That Monday, as the automatic doors whooshed open and she rattled her cart over the threshold, of course with one crazy wheel spinning wildly, he was there, leaning against the newspaper rack in his skinny jeans, a greasy smirk on his lips and a fresh fat whitehead glistening on his downy upper lip. *Derek.* The bag boy who squished her bread, busted her eggs, and worst of all always slipped in a few plastic bags although Rita clearly expressed her preference for paper. *Derek, the dirtbag.*

Jacob was already straining against the cart's seatbelt, arching his back and grunting. Rita estimated she'd have less than ten minutes before he managed to turn himself completely around and get into his rear-facing kneel. Abigail was clinging to the back of the cart, weighing her down on the turns as she tried to blast through the produce department with record speed, choosing vegetables based solely on their proximity and lack of need for bagging. *Fuck the green beans, fuck the Brussels sprouts. Nobody likes them anyway.* Rita accidentally smacked Abigail in the nose with a tossed eggplant, and she started to cry. Rita flew toward the bakery aisle, grabbing a baguette. She loaded two packages of ground beef and an 8-piece cut-up chicken into the cart in one graceful swoop with no change in velocity. She started muttering to herself as she plowed down one aisle and up the next. *Have olive oil. Need ketchup, need Cheerios, need bouillon cubes. Apple juice, cheese sticks. Shit, go back for teabags.* She rounded the corner past the pork 'n' beans endcap and slid into the check-out lane just as Jacob was hanging his head over the back of his seat, his poufy bottom poking toward the fluorescent lights and metallic balloons hovering overhead.

And there was *Derek*, propped on one scrawny elbow, whispering something to the cashier as she cracked her gum and narrowed her heavily-lined Cleopatra eyes at Rita. *Paper or plastic?* she asked, stifling a little giggle. *PAPER.* Rita enunciated it clearly. The girl started swiping Rita's items with a bored sigh. Derek slid her 8-piece cut-up chicken into a plastic bag.

Usually, Rita would let herself simmer. Usually, she would wait until she'd loaded all the bags into the back of the station wagon and buckled the kids into their car seats, then she'd slam her fist into the steering wheel and spew a string of choice words that Jacob would repeat in sing-song chant all the way home. But on this day, as she reached into her back pocket for her bank card, she grasped Zoltana of the Borderlands.

HEY she said, loud enough that shoppers in neighboring lines turned and gawked *I command you to use the paper bags.*

Derek's jaw dropped, spittle glistening on his lip ring. *What? You WHAT me?*

COMMAND. I said I COMMAND you to re-bag my groceries as I desire.

Are you fucking crazy? Derek balked. *Who do you think you are, lady?*

Rita seized the long paper sleeve of her baguette in her left hand, and grasped the crusty butt of it in her right. She unsheathed the bread in one deft motion, raising it high above her head. She raised her chin and spoke *I am Zoltana of the Borderlands, and I will kick your punk ass from here to the underworld if you do not bow to my demand. I will also tell your manager that you dropped an f-bomb.*

Jesus Christ said Derek, pulling the 8-piece cut-up chicken from the plastic bag. *Take it easy, okay?*

Rita wheeled her groceries out to the station wagon with a triumphant grin on her face. Abigail was swinging the baguette in front of her, making lightsaber noises, and Jacob was cheering. An elderly lady sidled up to her as she was leaning in to fasten the seatbelt across Abby's booster.

Good for you, sweetie the woman whispered. *That kid Derek is a little prick.*

Rita noticed that her symptoms were lessening. Maybe it was the supplements, maybe it was the hormone cream. Her periods were almost reliably normal. She was sleeping better. She found that she had more patience with the kids, and she was experiencing remarkably less under-boob sweat.

And then, as the proverbial April showers began dampening her world, holding her and the children hostage inside the house with greater frequency, Rita realized that once again, the annual descent into her very own personal hell had once again snuck up on her. The invitation appeared in the mailbox on the Wednesday afternoon before the dreaded event.

Please join us this Saturday at Chuck E. Cheese's to celebrate Veronica's 6th birthday!!!

Her husband's sister Gwen always sent the invitations at the last minute. And she always defaulted to Chuck E. Cheese's. It was bad enough when parents couldn't just have cake and ice cream at their own damn houses with little fanfare, but Gwen went above and beyond, requiring that every year, her guests be subjected to a gruesome gauntlet of eardrum-bleeding electronic noise, pizza-fueled hysteria, a crazed orgy of flashing lights and juvenile nervous breakdown. It was what Gwen considered fun. There would also be, without fail, at least a few pictures snapped just as Rita was shoveling a mass of birthday cake into her mouth, or bending over at an unflattering angle to tie a shoe. Pictures that would be gleefully uploaded to Facebook with haste, and tagged to make sure that everybody Rita knew would get a good look before she had a chance to untag herself while muttering expletives and chugging her traditional post-perdition beer or two. Or three.

Veronica's sixth birthday party was, unsurprisingly, as appalling and traumatic as all those that had come before it. The animatronic rock star mice were terrifying to Jacob and he cried until he puked pepperoni pizza onto Rita's lap. Abigail spent the first hour with her hands clamped firmly over her ears, repeating *It's too noisy, Mama, it's too noisy.* When she finally acclimated to the roar and ventured out into the roiling pit of frenzied children and blinking, flashing, beeping, ringing video games, she promptly climbed to the top of the indoor play structure, panicking inside a closed plastic tube. Rita stood below, watching feebly, as Abigail's face appeared in the bubble window, her mouth warped to the gaping proportions of a horror-movie scream, her eyes wide with all-consuming fear. Rita knew that she was shrieking her head off up there, but she was strangely fascinated by her silent view of it. Well, silent but for the deafening din swallowing her alive. She stood entranced. It was kind of like an underwater torture ballet. Vomit was drying on the crotch of Rita's mom-jeans. Abigail's face was kind of purple.

Rita found herself pondering how she might have drawn the scene, back when she was an artist. She imagined it stylistically as Egon Schiele might have rendered it, but, you know, without any pubic hair or hookers. Warbling lines, distended face, surprises of color.

And then Rita sneezed. She flew to the restroom to see what new prize had materialized. There, squatted over a grungy toilet bowl in the depths of Chuck E. Cheese's, while her daughter remained trapped like a half-witted gerbil on the ceiling and her son was doing god-only-knows-what, Rita pulled a purple crayon from her vagina. She smiled, tears souping her eyes. She had carried that nub of purple crayon with her everywhere, wanting to be just like Harold. It was little Harold and his magical purple crayon that had made her want to be an artist in the first place.

I've been thinking about this for a while—Rita started.

Yeah, me too her husband said, running his fingers through her hair and guiding her head back down to the matter at hand.

No she said *not THIS. Something else I want to talk about.*

Of course. You do realize that chatting and blowjobs are pretty mutually exclusive, right?

Well, I thought we could just take a little break here.

A little break? What if while you talk you use your hands?

Okay, deal. The thing is, I want my own room.

What do you mean you want your own room?

I don't have any space of my own. I don't have any place to put my personal things, or space to do my own projects. You have the garage all to yourself, and the basement too. I want a room.

Isn't that what the kitchen is? Your room? Ouch!

Rita decided that Abigail would have to sacrifice her room to a higher cause. The guest room would be renovated into a shared bedroom for both kids, and Abigail's little room would become Rita's new studio. She hauled out all the furniture and toys, and started stripping off the Hello Kitty wallpaper. Abigail stood in the hall and cried. Jacob rattled the bars of the baby-gate that she had installed at the doorway. Rita turned up the radio to drown them out and started painting the walls a rich red that she'd picked out the previous Sunday. It was not lost on Rita that it was a particularly menstrual color, although when she'd first started perusing the crimson shades at Home Depot that had been only a subconscious glimmer.

There was just enough room in the studio for a bookcase, a couch, and Rita's easel, which had been collecting dust in a corner of the attic since she'd been pregnant with Abigail. She'd squirrelled it away with the worry that the fumes from her oil paints might be harmful to her bellyful of baby. But she hadn't just stopped painting with oils. She'd stopped drawing too, stopped everything.

Rita moved in all her things and sat, gazing at the bare canvas. She centered the painted miniature and the purple crayon on top of her bookcase. She didn't want to leave her room that night. She stretched out on the couch, and she drifted in and out of slumber comfortably, opening her eyes every so often just to look around with satisfaction.

VAGINAL DISTURBANCES

Rita's first two paintings were kind of shitty. She knew it. She'd worked on them little by little, when the kids were in bed for the night. She'd carved out scraps of time from their days, collected crumbs of minutes for brushstrokes while Abigail and Jacob fitted their chunky wooden puzzles together, or shot Little People from the cannon of the Fisher-Price pirate ship, on the hallway carpet. She painted vaginas, of course. Well, vulvas. Vulvas in shy drag, trying to pass for flowers or landscapes. The specter of Georgia O'Keeffe hovered heavily over Rita's palette, dipping her faraway fingers into the linseed oil. They were demure vulvas, creamy and dreamy vulvas. Rita was not satisfied with these vulvas.

She wanted to paint a vulva that was heroic. Bold. Vigorous. Brutal in its raw power. The kind of vulva that would hit you like a muscle car of pure sun-smacked gold careening wildly over the edge of reality. A vulva that could slam you against a wall and steal your milk money, leaving you with scars. The kind of vulva that would strangle you with transcendence. The kind of vulva that was a flaming Vesuvian ball gown, with a blasting heart of living fire. A vulva that would scorch your eyeballs if you looked at it dead on, like the radiant ring of a solar eclipse. A vulva that would singe your eyelashes and make you hear classic rock as covered by a full symphony orchestra.

Rita wasn't sure how she was going to accomplish this. She prepared a new canvas and penciled a rough sketch. A vulva wreathed in fire, a wanton sister to the Sacred Heart. But there was something vital missing, some essential spark that was eluding her. Even as she pondered the potential colors, mused over the texture, she knew that her design was flawed. Incomplete.

Did you think we were done?

Rita's husband looked up from between her thighs.

Um…well, I'm kind of still working on it. You couldn't tell?

No, I mean, did you think we were done having babies?

Oh. Well, kind of, I guess so. You said you weren't really into the idea of cranking out another after forty. Didn't you say that?

Yeah.

Rita's husband sat up and looked at her. His face was soft and serious in the lamplight.

Have you changed your mind?

I don't know. My feelings are strongly ambivalent.

Well, if you don't care, why—

Don't be a dumbass. "Ambivalence" is not "apathy." "Ambivalence" is being torn.

Oh, right. So you might want to keep trying?

I don't know if it's possible now. And I don't know if I'd even want it. Kids are so amazing, but they also just suck so much.

They both laughed. He pinched her hip, she nibbled his collarbone.

I guess I just thought that it might be three. I don't know. If we're really done—

We could try.

Two is probably really enough, you know. I just feel like I need some kind of closure, maybe. Suddenly my insides are all haywire and things are just all weird in there. I'm not ready to be a crone.

You are not a crone. You are still super hot.

Rita's husband kissed her. It was a really good kiss. He wrapped his arm around her, pulled her head into the comfy space of his armpit. She loved the smell of him. Peppery. Like those cheddar cookies her mother used to make at Christmastime.

I understand, I do, he said. *It's like your stupid box of socks.*

What?

All the socks. You're hanging on to all those single socks, waiting for the matches to turn up. But they're not going to magically reappear. You just need to let them go. Like you said, closure.

My stupid box of socks. Rita thought about it for a minute. *You are a genius!*

Yeah? Yeah, I am. You know what geniuses really like?
They don't give out blowjobs at Mensa meetings.
They totally do.

Rita had made a belly cast when she was pregnant with Abigail, wrapped her ripe abdomen and swollen breasts in damp gauze and smeared them thickly with plaster. She'd planned on painting it, but it had languished in the attic for years. She'd bought another kit to make a cast during her second pregnancy, but never got around to using it. It was squirreled away in a drawer with Jacob's completely blank baby book. She needed the cast now, and the kit. And that stupid box of socks. She constructed a custom canvas, a huge one, and mounted the belly cast on it. Then she started plastering the socks, creating the bulging asymmetrically graceful lips of the three dimensional vulva that would bloom beneath the molded curve of the cast's pubic mound.

The color started as a deep purple at the shoulders, fading gradually over the breasts into violent violet and then a misty mauve that swerved and swept over the hill of the belly, plunging into pink as it suffused the vulva. Then it burst into coppers and reds, the vulva winged with fire that lifted off the canvas in great feathers of conflagration. Subtle shadows, glimmers of starry consecration. Depth, complexity. Wilderness unspooling from the scarlet center, the vaginal heart that flared with fierce love.

Rita worked on her project for weeks. Her every breath was drawn from it and returned to it. She wore the same spattered and smeared denim overalls each day, the stains proliferating, their colors permuting. Even when she was wiping asses or brushing tiny teeth or mixing tuna fish salad, she wandered in the haze of its creation. She grinned. She danced in her socks on the kitchen floor with the children, slipping and sliding, thinking of color and viscosity.

Finally, one night when Abigail and Jacob were tucked into bed, dreaming happily, and her husband was unfurling roots into the couch downstairs, a beer in his fist and the television flickering hypnotic blues across his drowsy eyes, Rita finished her piece. The flaming vulva of remnant socks was completed when she affixed Zoltana of the Borderlands in her place of honor, springing forth from the vivid mystery of the vaginal mouth, her sword raised and her armor gleaming, and installed her precious purple crayon above, to be the clitoris. Rita laid back on the hardwood floor of her sweet little studio, pushing her hands deep into her overall pockets, and looked at what she had made. It loomed above her magnificently. Her belly rumbled with pleasure and her heart drummed out a slow and steady reggae song of utter satisfaction.

It was at that moment that Rita felt the first contraction.

She locked the bathroom door behind her. She was in labor. There was no doubt, she'd been there twice before. The hot pain pulled from her womb, radiated through the small of her back. Rita danced her hips in wide circles, stretching through the spasms. She started filling the tub. Twice she'd done this, but never by herself. She'd read about those mothers who did, scampering off alone to dark rooms discreetly, like gravid cats, pushing out babies in unattended quiet. Mewling kitteny babies. She'd thought she could never do such a thing. But she was aware that she would have to do it now. A calm certainty swelled in her.

Rita moaned. She sweated. She squatted heels to haunch in the warm water of the bathtub and gripped the porcelain with animal hands. She howled. It was a miracle she didn't wake the kids. Her husband knocked softly on the door.

You okay in there?

I'm awesome! I'm awesome, don't worry!

Uh, alright. Do, do you need anything?

Got everything I need. It's cool. Rita's voice broke into a feral groan. *Be out soon!*

She heard him retreat, the stairs creaking under his diffident footsteps.

And then Rita was in transition, wave upon wave of searing agony, with no pause between. This was the part in Abigail's birth when she bit a hole clean through her husband's favorite flannel shirt, leaving him with a crescent scar that he still proudly showed off to his buddies. The part in Jacob's birth when she loosed a hailstorm of obscenities on the midwife and accused her of vile witchcraft, announcing that she'd have certainly been burned at the stake in a time of lesser enlightenment.

She felt the urge to push. So she did. Rita pushed, tears streaming. Rita pushed.

And they started to break through, issuing forth one after another, sliding into the water like soft and boneless fishes of every possible species. Cottony fish, wooly fish, fleecy fish. In every color, in every size. Rita gripped the plastic shower curtain and stared spellbound as her bathtub filled with every lost sock that had ever ghosted away from her. Baby socks, toddler socks, husband socks, mama socks. Ones with little bows, or ruffles of sweetness. Ones with reinforced toes. Striped, argyle. A Hallowe'en sock with smiling black cats. A Christmas sock with perky evergreen trees. Matches for every sock she'd used to shape her majestic volcanic vagina, and many more besides. Rita panted, exhausted, when it was finished. She pressed her forehead to the cool tiles on the wall.

Fuck Rita said. *Now what am I going to make with all of THESE socks?*

And she laughed. She laughed long and loud. Her laughter pinballed through the house, smacking every surface until she could hear the children wandering groggily in the hall, and her husband cooing at them to go back to sleep. She toweled herself off and emerged from the bathroom smiling.

C'mon she said. *Let's all get in the big bed together.*

Rita burrowed in among the jumble of warm arms and legs, and listened to her family breathe. Jacob latched onto her nipple and gurgled contentedly. Abigail cuddled into the small of her back. Her husband eased his arm around her waist. The windows were open in the bedroom, the breeze tickled the curtains.

Rita closed her eyes and slept well. She dreamed of her birthday cake. It was delicious.

Chana Finkelstein made a golem baby

Chana Finkelstein made a golem baby. She was washing beets in her kitchen sink when she got the idea. The beet roots always had clumps of clay clinging to them. She held that first little glob of clay in her hand, and the heft of it was a bright pinprick of surprise. It was substantial, dense, like a dream when every word is weighted. She rolled it between her palms, and it became a snake. The snake whispered to her, *adom*, red. Her Hebrew wasn't so great, but she knew from her years teaching Sunday school. *Adom*, red. *Dam*, blood. *Adama*, earth.

Adam, the first man, fashioned of clay.

She thought about how God must have felt, fingering that first bit of slick, heavy mud. She imagined God hollow-bellied, with sterile stars for eyes, like herself. She and Mordy had tried for years. They didn't even talk about it anymore, but she felt that keening in her kishkes whenever friends in the mahjongg club showed pictures of their grandbabies, little bundles of plump flesh squeezed into *I ♥ My Bubbe* onesies. Chana rubbed the snake into a sphere, and dropped it into a Mason jar. She screwed on the top and placed it on the windowsill, among the little pots of aloe vera and the avocado pits spiked with toothpicks. She went back to the farmers' market for more beets.

Her collection of clay burgeoned in steady increments, and her refrigerator began to fill with jars of pickled beets. It didn't really seem so odd. Lacto-fermentation was all the rage. Everybody was talking about probiotics. Hilda Greenblatt was famous for her kimchi. Sadie Schwartz made garlicky green beans. Now Chana bestowed jars of beets on all the neighbors, and she and Mordy ate them at every meal. Mordy said he'd never been so regular.

When she had six jars of clay, she started on the sculpting. She wasn't very good at it, but she spent time each night working at the kitchen table, her cheetah-print reading glasses perched on her nose. She carved with a paring knife from the set that she'd won at a Sisterhood raffle in 1989. Mordy would ghost by on his way to the refrigerator for another can of beer, shuffle back to the television set. He wasn't one to ask a lot of questions.

Meanwhile, she started thinking about how she'd go about bringing the baby to life. She'd taken a class on Kabbalah a few years back at the JCC. Jewish Mysticism, taught by one of those Chabad rabbis, the wild-bearded ones who stand outside the baseball stadium, ferreting out the lapsed and the unaffiliated, urging the men to wrap their arms in tefillin. She found her notes and the slim textbook on one of the bookshelves in the den. She thumbed through the pages one morning while Mordy was golfing with Joe Lipschitz. There were a lot of diagrams depicting God as a tree of circles, and she reread some interesting bits on meditation, and even reincarnation. But there was no practical instruction to suit her needs.

She started going to that young Rabbi Kleinman's Lunch-and-Learn class on Wednesdays. After each session of exploring the relevance of the Genesis narratives in our Modern World and heaping paper plates with mounds of creamed herring, Chana would scour the synagogue library for clues, belching onion discreetly amid the stacks. Most of the books were biographies of Jewish celebrities and Yidded-up self-help schlock, but there were a few scarred hardcover volumes, dust jackets long gone, that seemed promising. She read her way through all the stories of the Maharal, Rabbi Judah Loew, who was said to have created a magical guardian from the clay of the Vltava River to defend the Prague ghetto from pogroms in the 16th century. There were reports from famous rabbis who claimed to have seen the remains of the golem in the attic of the Alt-Neu Synagogue. But there were other stories as well, the golem of Chelm, the golem of Vilna, and a whole host of folktales from across Eastern and Central Europe that were dismissed as bubbemeises, old wives' tales.

Chana surmised that the one thing constant in the accounts was that the creatures were animated by using one of the names of God. There were seventy to choose from. *Of course, why make it easy?* The Hebrew letters were written out on parchment or a little clay tablet and placed in the mouth of the golem, or else inscribed directly on its forehead. There were also vaguely described "incantations" and rituals that accompanied the act. None of the authors were forthcoming with the specifics. So she decided she would at least start practicing her penmanship.

She bought a notebook at the Rite Aid, and started filling it with lines of alef-bet, scrawled as neatly as she could manage, what with the touch of arthritis. By this time the golem baby was looking not-half-bad, and it sat like a centerpiece on the kitchen table, presiding over her efforts as a scribe. *A real honest-to-God sofer* she thought. *Well, soferet, since I'm a woman.* She wasn't sure there really was such a thing, a lady scribe, wasn't sure such things were allowed. If there were, she was sure they weren't old ladies at kitchen tables; they'd be the kind of hot-to-trot young women who went to beardless Rabbi Kleinman's shul, the kind who wore men's prayer shawls with miniskirts and dragged the tzitzis on the floor when they walked, stomping on the fringes with their hooker-shoes. Chana wanted no part of that.

But she was proud of herself nonetheless, and the baby looked on. She'd decided to give the baby eyes, pressing two dried chickpeas into the shallow sockets she'd thumbed out for it. For him. She'd decided it would be a boy, Adam. Adam Finkelstein. *Adam ben Chana.* She liked the sound of that. Mordy seemed spooked by Adam. He gave the kitchen table as wide a berth as he could; he kept bumping into the china cabinet, making all the plates and menorot wobble.

But Adam sat unperturbed, as Chana printed the names of God, right to left. Sometimes she'd still be hard at work after the Action 11 Late News was over and Mordy was ready for bed. He would clear his throat, use the downstairs toilet, leaving the door open so the flush would resound through the quiet house. The pipes would wail forlornly as they always did after use, and he'd drag his slippers on the hardwood floor. Sometimes she would relent and climb the stairs behind him, but more often she would shoo him off.

Finally, she felt she was ready, and she wrote out a name on a small scroll. It was flawless. She chose the tetragrammaton, the four-letter name that was so holy that it could never be spoken except by the High Priest, inside the Holy of Holies, on Yom Kippur. She figured an inscrutable, unpronounceable name should be the most powerful. She carefully sliced open a mouth for Adam and inserted the name, pinched his lips gently back together. She smiled at him. She stroked his lumpy head. She would still need to figure out a prayer to make her plan work.

First, she tried going to Rabbi Kleinman for help. His office was big and air conditioned, with leather couches and Chagall prints on the walls. When Chana explained her business, the young Rabbi looked at her as if she'd sprouted a Hitler mustache.

Mrs. Finkelstein he said, his eyes horrified. *You know these stories are fairy tales, right?*

Eh said Chana. *Who are you to say? Who am I to say? Can't you just help me find the right words?*

Rabbi Kleinman rubbed his smooth chin. He fiddled with his cufflinks.

Have you talked to Mordy about this? Have you been seeing your physician regularly, Mrs. Finkelstein?

Chana did not like the implication. She was not crazy.

You are no help at all, you little schm—

Mrs. Finkelstein!

Chana got to her feet, clutching her handbag to her bosom. Rabbi Kleinman raced to open the office door for her as she turned her back to him and stomped toward it.

Oh, don't bother. Do a good job at my funeral. I'll see you then.

Wait! Wait, Mrs. Finkelstein! Look, I'll give you this.

He slid a book off a shelf. *Sefer Yetzirah.* The Book of Creation. Chana had read of it in several of the books she'd recently inspected in the synagogue library.

You've heard of this?

Chana nodded.

Rabbi Kleinman shrugged his shoulders. *I guess it couldn't hurt anything.*

Thank you, Rabbi. I'm sorry about the, ah, the name calling.

She took the book in her hands reverently.

Please, Mrs. Finkelstein. Let me know how everything's going, okay? We can talk any time.

Chana tried. Every night for a week, once Mordy was snoring rhythmically in bed, she slipped out to the garage with Adam bundled up in the threadbare beach towel she'd always taken down to The Shore. She'd lay him out and recite passages from the Sefer Yetzirah. She tried bits that seemed pertinent. She tried lines at random, flipping through with her eyes closed and stabbing at the print with one finger. But nothing worked. Adam's chickpea eyes stared blankly.

So, she visited the Chabad rabbi. Rabbi Schechter's office was the size of her half-bath, and he was sweating profusely. Chana was nervous, but she told him everything. Rabbi Schechter was verklempt. He couldn't choke out a word for a full minute.

This, this is shocking, Mrs. Finkelstein he finally sputtered.

Yes, well, shocking as it may be, I need to make this golem baby. I think you'd be able to help me, right?

Rabbi Schechter took a deep breath. He hesitated.

Of course right. I knew it. What do you know?

Mrs. Finkelstein he said. *I cannot help you with this. To study such things, it's—*

Yes, yes she said. *I know it's not usually done, but—*

Mrs. Finkelstein, with all due respect, this is the sort of study done by very learned scholars, very learned men—

Ah, men. Scholars. I see. But I've worked very hard, Rabbi. And my Adam—

Adam?

The baby. Adam. He needs to live. I need him to live. Her voice cracked.

Rabbi Schechter shook his head sadly. *Pray to Hashem, Mrs. Finkelstein. Pray for a child, and perhaps you too will laugh with joy in your old age, like Sarah Imeinu, when she found she was with child.*

Like Sarah Our Mother Chana said. *Yes, yes I see. You won't do a thing for me.*

She was too sad, too tired to even bother with proper insults.

If not like Sarah, then like Chana, your namesake. Think of Chana, she too was barren and Hashem answered her prayers.

Yes she sighed. *But which ones work?*

Chana figured it out while in her kitchen, following the family recipe for gefilte fish. She was mincing the carp when it struck her. The pot full of heads was bubbling on the stovetop, and her mind had wandered to wondering how many logs of molded fish she'd made in all these years she'd spent in the kitchen. How many loaves of egg-washed challah, how many pots of chicken soup glistening with golden baubles of schmaltz? Oh, and to think of the number if she added in all those made by her mother, her grandmothers…

Chana dropped her knife onto the cutting board, and she ran for the attic stairs.

She found the box behind all of Mordy's piles of junk. Her mother Rose Stromberg, of blessed memory, had presented the box to her. Inside was all that was left of Chana's grandmother's possessions. Her immigration papers, her recipe book. Her siddur. But it wasn't *that* prayer book she wanted. Not the official siddur, not the one that Zelda Itzkowitz, of blessed memory, would have carried with her to shul every Shabbos, murmuring the Hebrew syllables by rote but never really understanding much at all. It was the little cloth-bound book of tkhines that she wanted, Yiddish devotions for women. These were the everyday prayers, written in the common language, that Zelda had understood. Written in the mamaloshen, the mother tongue, they were truly the prayers of her mothers. Chana felt in her bones that this had to be the key.

She'd never learned Yiddish, of course. There were still Hasidic families teaching it to their children as a first language, and speaking it fluently among themselves, but nobody modern took it seriously anymore. All of the great Yiddish literature, the novels and plays, were lost. Sure, Singer was translated. He'd won a Nobel. In 1978; Chana remembered it well. But even then, Yiddish was considered an embarrassment. Everybody was busy resurrecting Hebrew, making it into a spoken language after centuries of merely liturgical use. It was part of Jewish pride now, part of loving Israel, to learn Hebrew, to forget about Yiddish. Yiddish was vulgar, Yiddish was for the unlearned. Yiddish was the language of Our Mothers.

But Chana knew now just where to go. She paid a visit to the Mikvah Lady, Miriam Leibowitz.

Miriam had been the attendant for the women's ritual bath for as long as Chana could remember. Chana had only visited the mikvah once herself, to immerse on the night before her wedding. She had just never really been that religious. She could never imagine herself abiding the observance, going every month after her menses, counting clean days and slipping away to the building behind the Orthodox synagogue under cover of night to dunk in the waters and emerge a new, ritually pure wife. Like popping out of a cake, but without the sugar frosting. It did always seem like it might be kind of exciting though, returning home to Mordy knowing that they'd be right off to bed. That it was a commandment. That no baseball game or episode of *M*A*S*H* could trump her marital needs. It always seemed alluring to Chana, but also a lot of bother. In any case, Chana was well past menopause now, and it would seem well past passion with Mordy, too.

But she knew just where to find Miriam Leibowitz in the middle of the day, and the next afternoon she went, the book of tkhines snug in her handbag. Miriam was not well past passion, even though she was at least as old as Chana. Miriam was infamous for her regular visits to the Shalom Gardens Hebrew Home for the Aged. She was a widow, after all, and it was known that she had a lunch date with a different eligible alter kocker every day. Excluding Shabbos, of course. That was apparently not only when God, but also Miriam Leibowitz, rested.

Racy rumors buzzed around Miriam's perfectly coiffed raspberry-red hair like a crown of bees, but she would not let her honor be besmirched by petty gossip. She comported herself with the utmost dignity, and she had on more than one occasion called out a bewigged lady or two for their loshen hora. In the aisles of Stan Fleishman's Kosher Market & Fine Deli Meats. Loudly. And in Yiddish.

Chana ran into her outside Arnie Glick's room that Tuesday afternoon. Chana asked to speak with her privately. They walked together, and sat in the shade of the oak trees, on the patio where Shalom Gardens erected their sukkah each fall.

So Chana began. *I seem to have gotten myself all mixed up in some mishegoss...*

While Chana talked, Miriam rummaged in her bag and withdrew a long cigarette case, the soft leather kind with a metal clasp at the top. She slid out an ultra-slim cigarette and lit it with a blue Bic. She directed the thin streams of gray smoke over Chana's head, not saying a word. Chana reached the end of her tale and looked at Miriam expectantly. Miriam snubbed out her cigarette on the flagstone at her feet, and then leaned in.

She whispered *El Shaddai.*

Chana drew back and looked at Miriam, puzzled, but then she gathered her wits.

That's one of God's names.

But did you know its root? Did you know that the Hebrew word for breasts is shaddayim?

That I did not know said Chana.

You've been calling on the wrong name, I figure. That's the name you write out tonight. And you've been asking for help in the wrong places, too. That Kleinman thinks you're as demented as Rochel Nudelman, bless her poor fercockt heart, and that Schechter, even if he does know something, he's not going to whisper a word of it unless you've got a schmeckie between your legs. Anyway, why ask a man how a woman should make a baby? Their golems are all brutes, what would you want with that? said Miriam. *Now let me see your Bubbe's tkhines.*

She looked through the little book, and then she tapped a prayer with the tip of her red-lacquered nail. She read it aloud, and Chana felt her veins swell, although she didn't understand a word. It was still the most beautiful poetry. Miriam translated it into English, then handed Chana the book.

So she said. *You learn this one. You say it every chance you get, every day, for a week. Can you do that?*

Yes.

Good said Miriam. *But remember this. Chana did not just say magic words to get a miracle from God. Chana prayed with kavannah. With intention, with fervor. So much so that the priest at first believed she was drunk. You remember?*

Chana nodded.

You learn this tkhine backwards and forwards until it's seared into your heart, Chana Finkelstein. And next Tuesday at midnight, you come to the mikvah.

Chana kept nodding.

Bring your son with you.

A little gasp, like a sudden bloom, passed Chana Finkelstein's lips, and she started to cry.

Nu, voos vet zein? Chana Finkelstein made a golem baby.

Valerie and the rat

When Valerie got pregnant the first time she didn't buy glossy parenting magazines and worry about things like the menace of soft cheeses and sushi, or whether or not to dye her hair. She had just buried her own mother, dead at forty-five from a quick and thorough cancer, and she felt such worries were silly when compared to other terrors. She started remembering awful things she'd read, like the part in a Vietnam veteran's memoir in which enemy soldiers cinched the ankles of village wives' billowy cotton pants and let loose venomous water snakes inside, so they'd have no way out but in. Or the part in a novel about shtetls in Russia where during a pogrom, Cossacks sliced open the bellies of pregnant Jewish women and sewed up live puppies or rabbits inside them in place of their murdered babies.

It was then that Valerie started dreaming about the rats. She'd wake in the night snatching breaths and feel the ghostly echoes of tiny teeth and needley claws burrowing into her belly. She'd feel the singe of an s-shaped afterglow upon her plumping thigh where a naked tail had slithered moments before as she slumbered. She'd hoist her bulk out of bed and stumble to the bathroom, gulp water frantically and pace the apartment floors, her bare feet treading the hardwood. She'd never seen a rat in the building, and her husband Jake disregarded her anxiety as ridiculous. *That's what you worry about, imaginary rats? Try worrying about the bill from the midwives* he said *Our insurance isn't covering any of it.*

The labor was difficult and long. Valerie was transferred to a doctor she'd never met and she found herself flat on her back, numb from the waist down, attached to cords and lines and feeds that led to shining machines. Finally, the doctor, whose name Valerie had trouble remembering after, slit her belly and lifted a child into the bright air. She couldn't see the baby from behind the green curtain. She could only hear the desperate mewling. Valerie's eyes pearled with tears.

But the baby was fat and hale, a daughter, with pink carnation cheeks and deep blue eyes that matched Jake's. They named her Annie, after Valerie's mother. Valerie didn't dream of the rats anymore, but every once in a while, as she teetered on sleep with the suckling tucked safely in her armpit, her mind would race with fear for Annie's minute toes. She would startle, waking the wee girl, and hush her with a lullaby and a milky nipple. Annie thrived, and eventually, Valerie didn't think of rats at all.

When she fell pregnant with her second child, Jake thought it was high time they abandoned their small apartment and bought a house with a garden and a garage. She agreed. They chose a sullied old Victorian further into the heart of the city. They could tell it had once been starlet-beautiful, although now the stairs sagged and the carpet was moldy. It was wrinkled, but it was affordable, and Valerie was smitten by its stained-glass windows and high ceilings. They got right to work on renovations. Fresh paint and enthusiastic carpentry made a world of difference.

Her son was still an apple-sized secret, easily concealed behind elastic waistbands and peasant blouses, when Valerie first spied the rats. She saw their silhouettes in the evening as they scurried like long and lithe trapeze artists across the power lines between houses. Valerie marveled that she was not gripped by fear so much as she was instantly inspired to ardent and militant defense. After the first sighting she walked the six blocks to the neighborhood hardware store immediately and bought out their stock of rat traps. She searched Craigslist that very night and found a large and ornery cat, a battered ginger tom with a half-ear and intact claws.

She checked the traps compulsively, but she found no corpses. The cat began to bring rigid mice and sad-angled birds to the back steps, but there were no signs that he'd battled any rats. However, as summer faded and the weather cooled, their presence in the house became undeniable. First, it was the sunflower heads Valerie had harvested from the garden and hung to dry on the back porch. She found seeds scattered on the wooden slats, the paper bags that had hooded them with their drooping faces slashed open. Then, the top of the hot water heater became littered with little black turds. She hadn't wanted to resort to poison. She'd worried about Annie getting hold of it, or the cat. She'd read about how bad it was for the wildlife that ate rodents, how it killed owls. Everybody likes owls. She decided that first she would try different bait in the traps.

Every day, she tried something new. Peanut butter, spreadable cheese, popcorn. Bits of hotdogs, raw hamburger. In the evenings when Jake got home from work and asked her how her day went, she would detail the times of day that she checked each trap, whether the bait had been eaten or not, what small new delicacy she had offered their uninvited guest.

He would laugh, squeezing by her as she stood soaping plates in the kitchen sink, and pinch her bottom as he made for a cold bottle of beer.

Are they stealing our electricity yet?

Oh! Annie exclaimed. *Like the rats of NIMH!*

Exactly! Jake said, his eyes sparkling. *Do you think our rat is a Justin or a Jenner?*

Shut up! Valerie barked. *I don't think you're very funny.*

Oh, Mama Annie teased. *Have you seen Mrs. Brisby?*

Do you see what you've started? Valerie said, throwing down her dishtowel. *Are you going to be laughing when a rat bites her face?*

Annie's smile crumpled and her eyes startled wetly. A sob escaped her gap-toothed mouth, spittle glimmering on her outthrust chin.

Jesus Christ Valerie, was that necessary? Jake said, scooping Annie into his arms and holding her head to his shoulder with one paw.

Valerie stomped out of the kitchen, tears fogging her own eyes.

You know Jake called after her *it could be wise old Nicodemus! He might have something important to teach you!*

The morning that Valerie finally met the rat, she was so far along that she couldn't fit between the end of the countertop and the pocket door to the basement while carrying the laundry basket. She had to park the plastic basket on the linoleum, and then back down a step or two, slide it to her, hoist it into her arms. She had to walk backwards, very carefully, until she got onto the landing, where it was wide enough for her to turn around with the basket in her arms. She'd been reminding Jake for two days to carry the loads of wash down to the laundry room for her, but he kept forgetting. The little portable radio attached by snarled wire to the copper pipes above the washer was blaring *Funky Town*. Valerie was annoyed with Jake's forgetting, and *Funky Town* somehow just made it worse. She turned on the landing slowly, thinking that navigating this descent would surely be the death of her, and there it was, just visible above the edge of the laundry mound avalanching onto her chest. It was big. Ash gray. With eyes like doubled Mars. It was hunched in a criminal stance, caught holding one of Annie's lost socks, a little pink one with ladybugs circling the ankle.

Valerie dropped the laundry basket and it tumbled down the stairs, spilling the wash all over the dusty wood and onto the concrete floor. The rat bolted. Valerie spun and scrambled on hands and knees toward the kitchen, her belly scraping the steps. She slid the pocket door shut with a slam and sat on the linoleum panting. She didn't venture back into the basement all day. When Jake got home from work, she sent him into the depths to retrieve the laundry. He came back waving a pair of Valerie's favorite panties, one of the few pairs that were still comfortable for her to wear if she rolled them down under her huge belly. They were black cotton. Jake held them up to his face, spreading the leg openings with his fingers, and peered through the ragged hole that had been chewed out of the crotch.

Looks like I missed quite a party today Jake laughed.

Valerie retched.

She left the puddle of bile on the kitchen floor for Jake to clean up, as she waddled fiercely out the door toward the hardware store. She only made it one block before her sciatica forced her to quit. She sat on the curb, her knees pulled up on both sides of her belly, and she cried with animal moans.

Jake rolled up in the station wagon, Annie waving to her mother from the booster seat, giggling. He sighed. *C'mon, get in.*

He drove her the rest of the way to the hardware store, waited in the car with Annie while she bought the poison. It sat on her lap in its brown paper sack as they drove home in silence, disturbed only by Annie's favorite song beneath her breath.

After bathtime and bedtime, Valerie made her way down the narrow steps and strategically placed the little green death bricks around the basement. She crept into bed that night exhausted, but it was impossible to sleep. She dreamed that the rat was swimming in the bathtub, its body sleek and slippery, twisting in the moonlight that fell in thin slices through the Venetian blinds. It slipped into her bed wet, tiny claw prints across her sheets. It squatted on her pillowcase, opened its fangy mouth to whisper in her ear.

Valerie woke in a cold paste of sweat, the baby quaking in her belly, no room to flip or turn. His elbow jammed into her ribs. She walked the floors until the sun came up, every quick shadow causing her to cringe. She couldn't stop thinking about the dream rat, what secret it might have slipped her if she hadn't escaped.

She made blueberry waffles for Jake and Annie's breakfast, but she couldn't eat anything herself. After they'd left for school and work, Valerie stood at the head of the basement steps, digging her fingernails into her palms. When she finally mustered the courage it took only three steps before she noticed the neat line of green rectangles. Each of the toxic bricks had been collected and arranged on the bottom step.

Every morning, Valerie took the baits from the bottom step and placed them in their proper spots in the basement. They kept reappearing, there on the step. She didn't dare mention it to Jake or Annie. Meanwhile, her pregnancy stretched on. One week past her due date, then two. She couldn't sleep, she couldn't eat. Her ankles were snakebite-swollen and her breasts hung heavy.

She checked in with her midwives by phone each day, and they smoothed her over with encouraging words, but Valerie cried whenever she was alone.

Why don't you just go ahead and let them induce you? Jake asked, making himself a sandwich, as she sat at the kitchen table with her head in her hands.

C'mon she said. *You know the dangers of that.*

Yeah he said *but you're already so far along. I'm sure he's done cooking.*

I'm not going to end up cut again. If he was ready Valerie said *he'd let me know.*

Valerie, don't be mad, but maybe you're the one not ready.

Valerie lay in bed that night, again unable to sleep. Her mind wandered to a painting she'd seen once, of the corpse of a mother who'd succumbed to the Black Death. The mother sprawled on the floor, pale and inert, arms limp, with her baby still suckling from her cold breast. A shudder passed through Valerie's body, slowly. Her bones bruised and her heart was wrecked. She whispered the word into her pillow, not knowing for sure to whom she was pinning it: Mama.

She made her way downstairs in her voluminous white nightgown, like a ghost, descending. She skimmed through the kitchen, just stopping to pull a paper bag from under the sink. She flipped the switch to the basement light and descended further, slipping underground, into the citrusy glow. Steadily, she collected all the poisoned bait in her sack. Then she settled on the bottom step and waited.

Okay Nicodemus she said aloud. *What do you have to teach me?*

The rat scuttled out of the shadows, and sat before her. It looked at her with its ruddy eyes. Then it opened its mouth, and out tumbled a small shining object.

Valerie heaved herself to her feet, sway-backed and slow. She knew what it was before she bent down to pick it up. It was her mother's wedding ring, *Annie* engraved inside the band. The ring that had been on her mother's finger when Valerie buried her.

Valerie slipped the glistening gold circle over the knuckle, onto her own finger. The rat scampered back into the shadows, and she watched its pink tail disappear. She filled herself to bursting with breath, closed her eyes, then loosed all her air until she was hollow. Her heart paused for one, crisply limned moment.

Valerie's waters broke.

The water

When it started to rain, we didn't know that it wouldn't stop. We didn't know that the sunflowers would bow under the weight of the water and kiss each other goodbye, that the horses would swim until they sank in surrender, that eventually even the wood of our crude boats would rot from underneath us.

Our arms would become pale eels and our eyes would dilate in the depths, but we didn't know it then. We stood under the banana leaves in the backyard, holding hands as the pattering began. Our fingers were braided and our breath smelled sweet as it raveled between us, binding lungs to lungs. We smiled at each other with flickering mouths full of sturdy teeth. We whispered each other's names; we used names then, we spoke them aloud and they traveled on air like dandelion parachutes. It was summer.

He pressed his palms to my swollen belly although it was too early to feel a kick. His hands were warm and dry, and the rain dribbling down over the edges of the leaves was cool as it hit my pinked shoulders. We gambled on the appearance of a rainbow.

We speak now only in dreams, drag memories to each other like our cats once offered small corpses on the altar of the cellar steps. He brings me the sound of cicadas, and I give him the taste of bread. He brings me our first kiss, the smell of marigolds, a snowy morning curled in bed with a paperback book. I give him driving at dawn in his gold Valiant, a sour swallow of beer on a humid afternoon, the baby's nursery filled with the origami cranes he folded for weeks. The patterned paper hung from fishing line, pointed wings spread; they floated on the morning sunbeams, a trick.

I went back down to the house. Our house, now a shipwreck. I drift through rooms, cling to the door frames, see precious things crumble and rust. He brings me fish in the evenings. I wait at the back window, watching the detritus of our lives tangle in the submerged treetops. A threadbare Black Flag t-shirt, his favorite wool socks, the feathers I collected and kept stuck in the neck of a brown bottle. The family Bible, spread open, ink washing from the pages, records of births and deaths trailing into nothing.

Little phosphorescent things curve themselves toward the surface, mingle with our belongings, rise through the pecan branches like fireflies once did. The glow is the same. He appears with fish in his hands. He cuts away the scales for me, I close my jaws on the raw flesh. The baby tumbles in my belly. His hair has grown long and he has a beard that sways like seaweed. I wonder whether we will lose our hair eventually, become as smooth as whales or dolphins. I wonder whether our fingers will web. I wonder if this baby will be human. He swims away into the black above and I know only that we will meet again soon in sleep.

He's brought me a memory of a spider's web, backlit by the porch light. There's no spider, just the silk strands, imperfect and shuddering. I offer him the radio playing in the kitchen while I slice into warm and bursting tomatoes. It was a Sunday, and he walked up behind me and put his hands on my hips.

I know you are looking for others. But I don't think there's anybody else I think, reaching to touch his shoulder with my knuckles. I want him to come home, I want him to haunt this place with me. I want him to stay. The baby will be born soon.

No, I'm not. I'm not looking for anybody else he replies without sound.

What are you doing then? I don't have to move my lips, but I do. I clutch his hand.

Searching for God.

Why?

Yes, exactly. Exactly.

I don't need to know. I am building a nest in the nursery. I am weaving driftwood, piling shells. The walls sag but my muscles have become hard. My ripe belly is a taut white ball. It hasn't grown heavy for me. There is no weight; the water cradles. Little fish tap at the window glass. Everything is quiet here, everything is undisturbed. The baby will not need a name. The baby will not need answers.

I free the dishtowels. They float away like jellyfish, they are whispers. I empty the house of linens, they twist like mermaids. Books, photographs, monarch butterfly wings released from their carved wooden box. They drift up.

One day, soon, I know he will not return. And the dreams will fade, the tether will snap. The child will be human, or not. But we will have the water.

Funny how tender can mean two things

〜

Lydia hadn't realized Paul's superiority to Kurt all at once. It hadn't been swift like food poisoning. It had crept up on her, a slow chronic cough. By the time she was aware of the idea's germination, she had already started wearing no underwear every time Paul came to dinner.

Lydia fantasized that Paul might bend her over the kitchen sink and rip open her blouse, scattering little pearl buttons across the linoleum. He would splash dishwater on her breasts with one hand as he hitched up her skirt with the other. Or maybe they would both be in the laundry room. Paul would lift her off her feet and seat her on the clothes dryer. It would be in the middle of a permanent press cycle, and the lid would would be hot against her bare ass. She'd grip the handle to the lint trap tightly, fighting the urge to bite Paul's neck. Lydia once imagined a scenario involving a big mixing bowl full of raw meatloaf mixture, but she didn't want to think about that again.

It was right after sunrise and Lydia stood at the kitchen sink in her pajamas, eating cold sesame beef out of a Chinese take-out container. She was looking out the window, watching her twin sister Penny emerge from her own house next door in her own pajamas. Penny circled the uprooted oak that lay toppled across the property line. She carried a big black open umbrella although the night's storm had wasted to a drizzle. She was wearing polka-dotted rain boots. It was high tide and half of their front lawns were ankle deep in water. That's what riverfront living got you these days. That and a fallen oak.

Sometimes, watching Penny from afar was like finding an old photograph of herself that Lydia had never seen before. Lydia's mind would glitch for a moment, trying to remember what it had felt like to be right there, right then, in the moment she was watching unfold. She didn't know if Penny ever felt like that. Lydia had never asked her.

Lydia and Penny had had a fairy tale double wedding, with two plastic blonde brides perched opposite two plastic blonde grooms atop a gigantic tiered cake. They'd married another pair of twins, Kurt and Paul, whom they'd met on a cruise for dental professionals. Lydia and Penny were both former dental hygienists, and it had seemed that they were destined for the Doctors Bishop, DDS. Everybody thought it was the most adorable thing. Their Instagram photos got *hundreds* of likes. Colleagues had fallen all over themselves making sure they were introduced on that cruise, encouraging them to eat their meals together. It was just luck that Penny sat down across from Paul at that first lunch, and Lydia faced Kurt.

They'd started planning the wedding right away. After the newly recoupled couples came back from their double honeymoon in Mexico, they moved into near-identical houses next door to one another. It had been prime real estate then, before the flooding got so bad. Lydia and Penny each planted a rose garden. Lydia and Penny each made casseroles, and ironed shirts. Lydia and Penny each got pregnant.

But Penny had a little girl, now almost 18 months old, with fat cheeks and curls, and Lydia did not. Lydia's blue baby never breathed. Lydia might have been able to forgive her sister for that, but she couldn't forgive Penny for being loved by Paul. Lydia was in love with her sister's husband.

The week after the stillbirth, while Lydia was writhing in bed with plugged ducts, Penny had brought her the gift of a canary in a cage. To cheer her. Lydia said *thank you* then hung the cage in the laundry room. She placed a blanket over the bird and went back to bed with her hot washcloths and sage tea. She was pumping just enough to relieve some pain, pouring out the milk into the bathroom sink.

Lydia did not feed that bird once. Each day, she measured out a scoop of seed into the downstairs toilet and flushed. Sometimes, it took two or three flushes to clear the bowl. By the end of the week, her engorgement had subsided and she took the cage down from its hook and deposited it into the outside trash can, blanket and all. Lydia felt no need to see the unpleasantness underneath.

There was a bit of sesame beef lodged between Lydia's first and second maxillary bicuspids. The beef gave her a dull, pleasurable ache. Lydia was in no hurry to floss. It was the same small delight she felt after a good rigorous dental cleaning, the same tenderness. Funny how tender can mean two things.

Kurt's alarm began to whine and Lydia left the Chinese on the kitchen counter, her fork poked inside the box. No doubt Penny would be over soon, wanting to discuss the fallen tree. Lydia had best attend to her morning ritual. She took the steps two at a time and slid into bed with Kurt before he'd had a chance to kick off the covers. She nuzzled her head into his warm armpit and slipped her hand into his pajama bottoms.

Wake up, little bird Lydia said, grasping Kurt's penis.

She wasn't sure if her ritual was religious in nature, or if it was practical magic. Every morning, she had an orgasm, and when she did she thought Paul's name. Maybe it was a prayer, or maybe she was casting a spell. She hadn't yet figured it out exactly, but it kept her sane. If she or Kurt overslept, or anything else interrupted routine, Lydia masturbated as soon as Kurt left for work.

Sometimes, she liked doing it alone so she could say Paul's name aloud at the moment of climax, whispering it to the bathroom tiles or into her sweaty pillowcase. It seemed to be more powerful that way, the prayer-spell. Like invisible threads left her mouth and burrowed through the walls of her house, traveled through the dirt under the sod and invaded his house, wriggling up through the floorboards and sneaking into his body through the pores of his skin. But, of course, it was also very easy to pretend that Kurt was Paul, as they were identical. So having Kurt do the work had its own attraction.

That morning, as Lydia arched her back against the mattress and bit her lip, silently screaming *Paul*, she was thinking of the uprooted tree. Last night, during the worst of the storm, Lydia had wished with great strain that the oak would fall and crush her sister dead.

Lydia was washing up Kurt's breakfast dishes when Penny came through the back door into the kitchen, the baby dangling from a carrier strapped to her chest. Her hair was still damp from her morning shower, and although she was still wearing her rain boots, she'd changed from her pajamas into a sweater set and corduroy pants.

So, wow Penny said. *I'm sure you saw the tree.*

Lydia dropped her sponge into the soapy water and wiped her hands on a dish towel, pressing her hipbone hard against the edge of the kitchen counter. It would leave a bruise. She was like fruit.

Yep. I'm going to call this morning to get some quotes on removal.

Penny sighed and hung her arms loosely. Her mouth was an arch, a colorless rainbow.

That tree always had rings of mushrooms around it, and when Clara was older I was going to tell her that it was a faerie tree. Penny nudged Lydia's shoulder. *You remember our faerie tree?*

Of course Lydia answered. *But we never saw any faeries.*

So what? The arch of Penny's mouth flipped. *It was the fun of it, you know.*

The baby started struggling to get free, so Penny busied herself unbuckling. As soon as her little socked feet touched down on the linoleum, Clara wobbled right over to the cabinet where she knew her Auntie kept the Tupperware and wooden spoons for her. Penny poured herself a cup of coffee and sat in the breakfast nook, scrolling through her emails.

Oh my God she said. *You'll never guess who's pregnant.*

I got the announcement too.

Lydia turned back to the sink and began drying plates with the dish towel.

Knowing her Penny said *she'll probably name it something like "Sundance" or "Remedy."*

Lydia often wondered, if she were to take Penny's place, would she be able to fool the baby? They were supposed to be able to smell their own mothers. Lydia had seen a video on YouTube of blind-folded babies correctly choosing.

Will you watch Clara while I run some errands this morning? After the tide goes out? Penny asked. Her eyes were still on her phone. She swiped with her thumb as she brought the coffee mug to her lips with her other hand.

No problem Lydia said. *I'd love to.*

She thought about how piping hot that coffee was.

Penny winced and blurted *Shit, I burned my tongue.*

It was hard to say exactly what made Kurt and Paul so different. Paul was in fact two minutes older and half an inch taller.

Lydia imagined that fucking Paul would be exhausting. That she'd be satisfied in the way that she'd been after digging out the withered rose bush. Or like she'd been when she finally got the dead baby out of her. It would be thorough. She would feel bereft in every cell of her body.

The tide went out and Penny left in her SUV. She'd be gone for hours. She always was when she had *errands*. Lydia suspected that Penny did that out of pity, to give her time with the baby. Or maybe it was spite. She was never confident in her ability to read Penny. Like with that canary. Penny was kind and happy, and something about that always made Lydia suspicious. People called Penny *genuinely nice*, and how could that not be some kind of scam? Lydia and Penny had never had one of those secret twin languages.

Clara sat on the living room floor and chewed on a board book version of *Where the Wild Things Are*.

Lydia stood watching the sunlight through the blinds catch in her golden curls.

I'll eat you up, I love you so she said out loud.

The guy came about the tree. He was young and bearded and wore a large belt buckle shaped like California. Lydia got on her rain boots and sloshed behind him across the spongy front lawn, holding Clara in her arms. The guy had his tape measure in hand, hooking its tang on various edges and muttering numbers to himself as he stretched out each yellow length and then let it snap back loudly into its coil. Clara was raising one hand to the sky, pointing a pudgy finger at the lingering storm clouds and babbling emphatically. Lydia was trying to listen to them both, trying to make sense of either. She felt a vertiginous spin and sudden beads of sweat on her upper lip. It happened so fast. Lydia's shin hit a protruding root. She tripped and fell, Clara tumbling from her grip as she tried to catch herself.

There was so much blood, and Lydia couldn't hear. There was a ringing in her ears. The ragged edge of Clara's mouth was flapping open. Surely she was screaming for her mother, howling in pain. The baby's right eye was obscured by blood that Lydia was scared to wipe away. She knelt on the swampy lawn, clutching Clara as her tiny body thrashed against her own in the strange vibrating quiet. Little hands scratched and pummeled. Lydia was moving so slowly as she tore open her blouse with one hand and brought Clara to her breast. Lydia rocked the child as she calmed, sucking on instinct at her dry nipple. Ambulance lights flashed but Lydia couldn't hear the sirens. When the EMT's tried to pry Clara from her arms, she snapped her teeth and tried to bite their hands. A needle plunged into her thigh through her wet jeans.

Lydia woke restrained. Her head was very heavy, and felt very round. She was afraid that her neck might be too brittle to support its weight. She decided to stay very still and think about Paul. He had a freckle on his neck that Kurt did not have. It was an island. It was a tiny speck of dry land.

Penny said *You can't blame yourself. It was an accident.*
She squeezed Lydia tightly, and then put her hands on Lydia's shoulders and peered into her face. Penny's eyes were swollen.

Lydia saw them as a snapshot. That picture of herself had been taken after the stillbirth.

She's going to be okay Penny said. *She had fourteen stitches and—*

She gagged on the words, covered her mouth with both hands.

And she lost her eye.

Penny screwed up her face hard, made fists at both temples. She doubled over, crying so forcefully that Lydia knew she would have constellations of burst blood vessels around her eyes. Lydia knew. She would see that picture of herself too.

She reached out her arm and touched the back of Penny's head.

It was an accident Lydia said.

She took a cab home from the hospital. It was high tide again and the car had to stop on the street a block further from the river. Lydia stood on her front lawn in her rain boots and looked at the tree. She looked at the two houses side by side, all windows dark. There were very small fish circling her ankles.

Lydia knew about the sleeping pills. Penny had been taking them since she'd weaned Clara. Paul was the one to get up every night to give her a bottle of formula, usually right around two. He turned on the light in the kitchen while he warmed the milk, and Lydia stood in her kitchen in the dark, watching. He was often shirtless. Sometimes he drank a glass of tap water. Sometimes he read something out of sight on the countertop. Sometimes Lydia put her hand under her pajamas and pinched a nipple.

Of course Lydia had a key to their house. She went straight up to the master bedroom and opened the medicine cabinet in Penny and Paul's bathroom. She swallowed patiently until all the pills were gone. She got out one of Penny's pink lipsticks and she wrote on the mirror *I love you Paul*. Then Lydia got into bed and laid her head on Paul's pillow with the empty bottle against her cheek.

Penny realized that her sister wasn't sleeping.

Oh my God she said.

Clara had fallen asleep in the car, and she was stirring in Penny's arms. Penny eased her onto her back on the bed next to Lydia. She turned the bandaged half of Clara's face toward the mattress, so that for a moment, she appeared unscathed. Like brand new.

When Clara was born, everybody else had been so happy. For those first few instants after the baby had been placed in her arms, Penny had felt happy too. But then she began to slide.

Oh my God she repeated. *Oh my God, this is it.*

Paul would be home soon. He'd said he'd be stopping off on the way home from the hospital to pick up Chinese take-out for dinner. So she wouldn't have to cook. Penny undressed her sister, and she undressed herself. She pulled on Lydia's leggings and cable knit sweater. She leaned over and kissed Clara good-bye. The kiss was tender.

As she hurried down the stairs to the first floor, Penny could hear the baby waking and beginning to cry. She locked the front door behind her and crossed the lawns in Lydia's rain boots. Of course Penny had a key to Kurt and Lydia's house. She went straight up to their bedroom. She got into bed.

Penny hadn't felt sleepy on her own in months. Exhausted, yes. But she never felt that sweet pressure of sleep pinning her to the mattress unless she took the pills. Without them, her body thrummed beneath the covers and her mind raced with doubts and dark things.

Now, Penny was so sleepy

No.

Correction.

Now, Lydia was so sleepy.

Rosemary & ghostmilk

Miranda woke in the dark, swamped by a puddle of warm and limp child-limbs. Her husband was snoring on the far side of the bed, but both of her sons were drawn in their sleep to her body only, the motherbody, their arms and legs reaching for the throbbing of her heart alone. She slipped free of their tangle, and rolled to the edge of the mattress. Miranda pressed herself to the wall. The plaster was cool against her sore and heavy breasts. They were full again.

  She descended the stairs with quick and quiet steps. She made her way through the kitchen with its steadfast blue pilot light and refrigerator hum, and out the back door into the garden. Miranda knelt in the dirt, feeling the damp soak through her nightgown to kiss her knees. She flattened her palms to the earth between the rosemary bushes, to the place where she had buried the blood and remnants of tissue that would have been her third baby.

  It had been a full year since she dug the shallowest of graves with her bare fingers. All the moons with all their poemy names had passed. And now, night after night, she woke brimming with milk, her swollen skin hot to the touch.

She had tried to rub out the memory of the cramps and clots. To clench her jaw and make those weeks spent denned down like a wounded animal under the feather blanket into a shadowy nothing. She had tried to unravel it and re-stitch a forgetting. Her heart became a walled city. But the tiny dinosaurs in the boys' birthday loot were the ram's horn that shook her mortar to dust, split her stones like the rinds of over-ripe fruits. Candy-colored reptile kings of superabsorbent polymer, designed to expand in water. *Grows to 500 times its original size!* Miranda had arranged a long row of quart-size canning jars along the kitchen counter, let the boys pour water themselves to fill them. They deposited dinosaurs into the wide-mouth jars, dropping them high from their pudgy fingers and giggling at each satisfying plop.

By the afternoon, the creatures had begun to swell. They floated, wispy and ethereal in their slimy coating. Looking through the water and thick glass, their shapes were distorted. Miranda felt a thrum of sickness in her belly. They were fetal. The line of jars whispered of preserved specimens, formaldehyde. Miscreations on sideshow display.

She snatched up one jar after another, her hands trembling, and dumped the contents into the kitchen sink. She averted her eyes from the viscous imps beached on the bottom of the stainless steel basin. One of the jars slipped from her wet fingers and shattered on the linoleum, and her sons came running to the sound. Miranda shooed them away, latching the baby-gate. Alone in the kitchen, she crouched and picked up the glass. The shards pricked her skin, her fingers bloomed blood.

That night, in the witching hour, she woke with her breasts engorged. Milk dampened the bedsheets. Every night that followed was the same, sleepless and sorrowing. While her family slumbered, she expressed by hand into the bathroom sink. Miranda burned, and she wept.

She took a pinch of earth from between the rosemary bushes and tasted it. It had the flavor of metal and salt, rain and rot. The grit between her teeth sang loudly in her skull. Rosemary is for the dead, rosemary is for remembrance. She'd known that when she chose the place in her garden for the burial. And yet, she had remembered only to forget.

There'd been no token to hold in hand, no lock of fine blonde hair or curled cord stump to place in a box. It had been too early for that. Too early for any substance to remain. Too early for condolences. Too early for anyone to understand the grief that weighted her emptied body, so Miranda had buried that too.

She tore a sprig from the rosemary and the night air was flooded with the fresh strong fragrance of it, piney and lemony. She held the woody stem between sticky fingers and began to pluck the tiny leaves, chewing them slowly, eating them one by one. She said aloud the names she had chosen. *Joseph* for a boy, *Suzanne* for a girl. She repeated them again and again, murmuring them down deep into the dirt.

And then, a rustle in the leaf litter. Soil disturbed, earth parting and opening. A pair of small slanted black eyes peering up at her from the underworld. Long soft ears, twitching and silvered in moonwash. A little rabbit hunched before her, unburrowed, unburied.

Mother it said. *Mother.*

Miranda loosed the laces of her nightgown and slid the pale blue cotton from her shoulders. Her bared nipples were stellar, singing in the dark. She gathered the creature into her arms and guided its hot and hungry mouth to her breast. It suckled. Milk gushed from her body, the motherbody, and her eyelids grew heavy. When the rabbit's belly was full, it dug back down among the rosemary roots. Miranda coiled herself around her own throbbing heart, and remembered. She lay in the dirt, between the rosemary bushes, and she dreamed of the rabbit circling the moon. Miranda remembered, and she slept.

The shearing of yossi mandelbaum

Upsherin (Yiddish, lit. "shear off") is a haircutting ceremony observed by a wide cross-section of Jews and is particularly popular in Haredi Jewish communities. It is typically held when a boy turns three years old. (Wikipedia)

Payos are the (often curled) sidelocks worn by some Orthodox men. *Tzitzis* are the fringes that hang from a four-corned undershirt (tallis katan, or "small prayershawl") worn by observant Jewish men. Boys traditionally receive their first tzitzis at the time of their upsherin.

On the morning of Yossi Mandelbaum's third birthday, his mother Leah woke with a killer headache. She'd been dreaming of sinking her teeth into a ripe pear, and of watching whales swim in the sky, weaving their improbably graceful heft between strings of comet tail. She sighed to remember the smooth arc of cetacean bodies, but cringed as the pain drummed on her skull. Even the dull light dribbling feebly through the Venetian blinds in her bedroom caused her eyeballs to burn, and the left side of her head thundered. Yossi had found his way to his mother's bed long before dawn, and now lay nestled against her soft belly, his thumb plugging his mouth, his long blonde curls spilling loose over the blue floral sheets. Leah shielded her eyes with one hand and reached with the other to stroke the wilderness of his hair. Yossi was her darling, her favorite among all of her children, although she would never have admitted to loving him more than the others. It had taken twelve years of trying, and five older sisters for Yossi, before she'd finally given birth to a son. She'd been dreading his upsherin, knowing that she would mourn the loss of his long hair, which now reached almost to the small of his back. She didn't have quite as much anxiety about it as she'd had over his bris, but almost. Almost.

Yossi rustled and the motion roused Leah's nausea. She groaned as the child climbed her, his little knees digging into her thighs, her belly. His weight, his full weight, was a ballast that held Leah in this world. She hated that, in a way, the banality of it. The stereotype of it, the cloying Jewish mother. All its saintedness and lack of surprise. The adoration of the son. But she felt it, she did, and knew that it was more than a metaphor when she thought of his weight pinning her to the earth. The truth was visceral, and her viscera knew: *Without my Yossi, I would float away.*

Yossi pressed his little bunny nose into the folds of Leah's neck. She wrapped her arms around him and squeezed. She pinched his tuchus and his fat little legs. She whispered into his ear, finding it hidden in his mess of curls. *Are you ready to get your big boy haircut today?*

I get a lollipop he said, the words slippery and spilling out around his thumb. The reverence in his tone was sweet, and so funny, although Leah succeeded in keeping her laugh caged in her chest. She gave a solemn nod. His seafoam eyes sparkled with anticipation. His joy tickled the back of Leah's neck and made her toes wriggle.

Yes, you get a lollipop while you sit nice and still to get your haircut.

Don't worrrrry about it said Esty Tendler as she smeared a knifeful of cream cheese across the top of a halved sesame seed bagel. *You'll love his little payos. You'll see, he'll be adorable.*

Oh and the little tzitzis! Rivvie Rabanowitz cooed, pulling two bottles of orange juice, one neck in each fist, from Leah's refrigerator.

I know, I know Leah said. *I love how the fringes are so long on tiny boys! It's so cute. And I know his payos will be sweet, too. It's just, you know, his hair is so beautiful, he's just so—*

Her voice crackled.

Oh now, don't cry Rivvie said, leaving the juice on the countertop and easing her big soft arms around Leah's shoulders.

Hey, it's okay added Esty. *He's not a baby anymore. That's hard.*

Leah nodded and sniffed. *Did I tell you we have Batman tzitzis? He's going to love it. Yehuda got fabric markers and drew the Bat Signal on it. He did such a good job, it looks like from a store, just perfect.*

Your husband the artist! Esty said. *This I can't wait to see!*

Leah sat on the closed toilet lid in the downstairs half bath. She'd taken four Tylenol when she'd gotten out of bed, but her headache was creeping back. What she wouldn't give to have a nice pear. Ah, but the nausea too was back when she thought of the fruit. Thrumming skull, roiling belly. There was a soft knock at the door.

You all right in there, Ima?

It was Leah's eldest, her daughter Yael.

I'm feeling a little sick she managed. She flushed the toilet. The water rushed under her and the pipes clanged. *I'll be out in a minute.*

Leah remembered the day, three years ago, when she first laid eyes on Yossi. The midwife almost hadn't made it there in time to catch him. Yehuda had been pacing in the hallway with his phone in hand, chomping at the bit, ready to call for an ambulance. After five previous births, Leah thought she'd known what to expect, but Yossi's emergence was like nothing she'd ever experienced. Yossi was a fireball, and when Yossi decided it was time for his much-longed-for appearance, he didn't waste a split second. The entire labor, from the amazingly audible loud pop of his amniotic sac breaking and that first dull pull through the small of Leah's back, to the final triumphant push that hurtled Yossi's finely formed soft skull into the midwife's latexed hands, took exactly a mere hour and forty-five minutes. Sarah Silver from next door had abandoned her kitchen mid-kugel when Yehuda had come banging on her door begging for help. Leah was on her knees on the bedroom carpet, gripping Sarah's shoulders so hard that the poor woman would bruise later, yelling out *That's crowning! I know what crowning feels like!* when the midwife came bustling through the front door of the house. Leah could hear her snapping on the surgical gloves as she took the stairs two steps at a time.

The funny thing was, Leah was almost disappointed that she didn't bear Yossi in that room all by herself. She was certainly thankful for Sarah Silver's support, and she was happy that Yehuda could feel like he was helping. The midwife had been shocked when Leah first informed her that her husband would not actually be present in the room for the baby's birth. She'd never attended for a religious Jewish family, and Leah could tell that although she was tolerant of their plans she didn't wholeheartedly approve. Leah had always liked having childbirth remain a woman-only event. She loved being surrounded by that feminine energy, she loved that it was a deep and gorgeous mystery of which Yehuda could have no portion. Leah loved her husband, but this, the act of creation, was something that was hers alone. Or almost alone. That was the ember that smoldered in her, that near-wish that she could have done it unattended. She imagined that she would have been just fine. She imagined that it would have been glorious, her face luminous like Moshe on top of Sinai. She imagined it would be like that, climbing the mountain alone to meet God face-to-face.

Leah checked her wig in the bathroom mirror, straightened her dark wing of bangs. She smoothed her dress over her hips. It was a very flattering new dress. Long sleeved green velvet, with just the right amount of cling, and a beautiful white lace collar and matching cuffs. She'd got it for 30% off, too. Leah smiled at her reflection, and she realized just then how much she looked like a lady from a Marc Chagall painting. Her dress, her dark bobbed wig. She could be a figure in his Paris, among flowers, or aloft over his Russia, green velvet trailing in her wake. Leah laughed. *What a thing.*

Rabbi Hirsch kept it short and sweet, *Baruch Hashem*, thank God, because the crowd in Leah's living room was unbelievable. The whole of Congregation Beth Israel must have been crammed in there. Leah was having trouble breathing. The Rabbi just talked a little Torah, then said a bit about how a boy leaves his babyhood behind, leaves the world of mothers for the world of men and mitzvot and learning. Leah pursed her lips and kept quiet. She and Yehuda took the first snips, passing the scissors between them, as Yossi sat in his booster seat happily sucking on a bright red lollipop. His lips were stained, and the blond curls tumbled down his back and fell to the cloth Leah had spread on the floor beneath him. She felt very light-headed, and her thighs were trembling as she handed the scissors off to the first guest in line. She crumpled into a folding chair and sat beside Yossi as each person took their turn at his head, dropping coins or stuffing tightly folded bills into the tzedakah box he balanced on his lap. Leah closed her eyes.

When she opened them, Yehuda was murmuring the blessing for tzitzis, and slipping the garment over a small boy's shorn head. Yehuda was placing a kippah atop that head. The boy was reaching for one of the aleph-bet cookies that Leah had baked, dipping it into the small dish of honey that sat on the cookie platter, and shoving the sweetness of Torah learning into his smiling scarlet mouth. This child, this giggling boy with golden payos, was eating the cookies she'd baked for Yossi. He was sitting in Yossi's booster, wearing Yossi's suit, beaming over the Bat Signal Yehuda had painted for his son, her precious boychik.

Leah sprang to her feet, gasping for air. *Yossi!* she shrieked. *Yossi, where are you?*

The room was dark, but Leah could feel the closeness and warmth of the women around her, smoothing her blankets and breathing softly. One of them, smelling like talcum powder, pressed a cool wet washcloth to her forehead and brushed damp ringlets of hair back from her cheeks. Leah could remember the ripple of laughter passing through the crowd as she called for Yossi. The laughter had turned sour, curdled to frightened whispers as the guests realized her frantic question was no joke. And then she had fallen, the faces around her fading to black.

There were murmurs now, and her tongue thick in her mouth as she tried to murmur back, asking for her boy. She could hear the vague clatter of post-party clean-up through the closed bedroom door. The rush of water into the kitchen sink, the stacking of plates and clearing of glasses from the tabletops. Cool fingers laced between her own as her voice creaked, her lips dry. She curled herself to sitting upright and somebody brought water to her mouth. She felt the cold of it all the way down her throat, felt the cold of it pool in her stomach.

Leah, how are you feeling? a voice asked. Maybe Rivvie. Leah's head was still fuzzy. It was hard to tell who flanked her.

What happened? she managed. *What happened to Yossi?*

Hands brushed her shoulders, her leg.

Yossi is fine, Leah. Yossi is just fine. He's adorable, as always.

That boy Leah sputtered. *That boy was not my Yossi.*

Oh, Leah.

They led the boy in, lighting the lamp at Leah's bedside. His short golden hair shined. His eyes were scared. He twisted his new tzitzis between his little fingers nervously.

Your ima is not feeling so well, Yossi. But she wants to see your handsome face. That will help her feel better, won't it Leah?

The boy shuffled forward. He reached out and touched the edge of the bedspread.

Leah could plainly see this was not her son.

Is this some kind of joke? she asked. *It isn't funny. Not at all.*

This is craziness! Craziness! Yehuda boomed. Leah had not even noticed him standing there, framed by the light of the hallway. His eyes were burning with anger, and Leah blinked at him hopelessly. The image of him swam, distorted by her tears. He strode into the darkened quiet of the room and snatched up the boy from her bedside in one swift and purposeful motion.

She just needs more rest one of the women bleated.

She needs a doctor Yehuda said, turning his back. The boy clung to Yehuda's shoulder tightly and let out a thin wail. It didn't sound like Yossi at all. Yehuda and the boy disappeared into the light, and Leah closed her eyes again. Somebody switched off the lamp. There was more whispering. Leah slept.

It was the middle of the night when Leah woke again. The house was silent. She didn't sense the presence of anybody else in the bedroom. She considered it and figured that Yehuda must be sleeping on the couch. No doubt he'd made an appointment for her to see Dr. Bloch in the morning. She would have to find Yossi before then. Before the dawn came and brought with it the bustle and noise. In the quiet dark, Leah's head felt clear. There was no more pain. She crept from the bedroom and down the hall, through the kitchen. Everything from the party had been cleaned up nicely. The house was in perfect order. The only thing missing was Leah's sweet baby. As she'd expected, Yehuda was stretched out on the unfolded sofa bed, his long legs dangling from the edge. There was a hole in one of his socks, his big toe protruding. Leah would have to remember to mend that.

The night was warm. Leah was still wearing her green velvet dress and didn't need a jacket. She walked along the pavement quickly, her eyes darting from house to house, hoping to catch a glimpse of Yossi at play on one of the neighbors' stoops or peeking out from behind one of the hedges. But there was no sign of him. The maple leaves were just beginning to come loose from their branches, and the moon was just a sliver. Another month, and it would be Rosh Hashana. Yossi loved the raisins in the holiday challah. He loved the apples dipped in honey, and the sweet carrot tzimmes. Leah called out his name softly as she turned the corner onto Belvedere Street. She scanned the trees that lined the curb. Yossi was just learning to climb trees, just getting good at pulling himself up by grasping the lowest branches. Sometimes, walking home from shul on Shabbos, she and the rest of the family would stop and wait at nearly every maple along the way, giving Yossi a chance to show off his new skills. He was better at it every week. But Yossi was not in any of the trees this night.

Leah saw a small dark object on the pavement ahead of her, half a block away. She broke into a run and scooped the item from the concrete. It was a small boy's yarmulke, lost. Blue, with silver trim and tiny teddy bears. She couldn't remember Yossi having a yarmulke like this one, but maybe it had been a gift today? She rubbed the satin lining between her fingers while her mind raced. It could certainly belong to Yossi. She ran, clutching the yarmulke to her breast.

She'd gone two more blocks, her neck twisting in every direction, her eyes glazed with panic, before she realized she was definitely headed toward the playground at the end of Belvedere. Of course. Of course Yossi would run there. It was one of his most favorite places. He loved to swing on the swings and slide on the slide. He loved to roll in the pine needles and chase the ducks around the perimeter of the pond.

Leah's heart dropped. No. No, not the pond. She screamed Yossi's name and kept on screaming it, again and again, as she ran, even faster than before. She didn't even notice the lights popping on in windows up and down the street. She didn't notice that her wig fell from her head, landing in the soft grass like a bird's nest fallen from an overhanging branch. She ran bareheaded and shrieking, thinking only of Yossi, only of holding him safe in her arms again.

Leah was on the little wooden footbridge when they found her. She had collapsed, still clutching the little blue yarmulke tightly. The pond glimmered in the dark, rippling with the tiniest of waves. She sobbed into Esty Tendler's arms.

He's drowned. I know it. He ran off and drowned and nobody even searched.
No, no dear Leah Rivvie whispered. *Yossi is well. Yossi is safe.*
You are so very confused Sarah Silver assured her, stroking her head.

Esty slipped Leah's lost wig back on and straightened it. She wiped at Leah's tears but they kept coming.

Sarah pried the yarmulke from Leah's grip. *This belongs to my Mendy* she said. *He lost it today when he was out playing stickball.* She tucked it into the pocket of her housecoat and reached for Leah's hands.

Leah pulled away. She pulled away from them all.

I'm alone she said. *I'm all alone without my Yossi.*

No, no Rivvie said. *You're not alone, Leah.*

I am Leah said. *I am alone. Without the weight of a baby to hold me down...*

You'll float away finished Sarah.

There was a deep moment of silence between the women.

Then the sound of footsteps on the bridge. They turned to look, and saw that it was more of the neighborhood ladies, women in their nightdresses, their unwigged heads bound up in terry cloth turbans and bright fringed scarves, slippers on their feet. Miriam Brownstein, a kind old bubbe who made the best rugelach, was standing in the center of the crowd, holding the boy in her arms. He was wearing footie pajamas, the ones that had been Yossi's favorite. White with little pirates all over, and pirate ships too. Yossi used to point and say *X! X marks the spot, Ima!*

The boy's shorn blonde hair was messy with sleep, the curls of his payos askew. His head rested on Miriam's shoulder. His thumb was planted firmly between his red lips. The woman walked him over to where Leah was sprawled on the wooden planks. She knelt down beside her.

Leah, please Miriam said softly. *Hold your son.*

Leah took the boy in her arms. She touched his mussed hair and stroked his cheek. She lay back on the planks of the bridge and held him against her tightly. His head slid into a perfect fit between her breasts. The boy sighed in his sleep. His thumb slipped from his mouth, and his little hand reached for Leah's neck. His grasp was moist and gentle.

He was sweet and soft and warm. But he wasn't Yossi.

The weight was just not the same. It was barely perceptible, but this boy was lighter. The difference was so slight, just the weight of a little golden hair.

The women gasped as Leah's back lifted from the bridge and hovered there, just inches above. Miriam took the boy back quickly, held him with her big safe rugelach-making hands, as Leah continued to rise, tears spilling like weird diamonds. She floated above the gathered mothers, in her green Chagall dress, her body a wisp, a curl of painted colors. She drifted, moving over the neighborhood, all the little houses in the dark below her and the moon a silver splinter stuck into the sky above. The women ran after her, their chins pointed up and their arms outstretched.

They scrambled up the curbside trees, their nightgowns and housecoats hitched, revealing their rosy knees. Branches snagged their tichels and turbans, and their hair tumbled loose among the maple leaves, blonde and brown and copper. They climbed high, and threw their hands out into the swirling sky for Leah.

Leah rippled and spun. She called out to them, her voice ringing like a bell. *I've got to go!*

No, no! The women called back, a chorus of bells rising to meet hers. *We will keep you!*

Leah saw Esty and Rivvie and Sarah, and the other balabustas, stretching themselves on tiptoes in the trees to reach her. She saw Miriam Brownstein cradling the sleeping child in her arms on Belvedere Street, petting his head softly and whispering into his ear as she looked up at Leah sailing above. The poor motherless boy.

Leah held out her hand.

They reeled her in, out of the sky. They piled their soft bodies over her, weighting her with their limbs and bellies and breasts. They kissed her eyelids and they held her hands.

Hold me down Leah whispered. *Yes, hold me here.*

The womanly art of drag racing

It was true that after years of IVF failure, Meredith had resorted to contacting Madame Ovary, but she was too embarrassed to admit that to the other moms in the La Leche League group. They were making fun of the commercials. Madame Ovary had been far less campy in person, but her late night two-minute appeals were definitely over the top. She looked like a sideshow gypsy, as if being a Licensed Fertility Witch was akin to reading palms and gazing into crystal balls. The moms were laughing and guessing that she must work out of the back room of a nail salon or a laundromat. But in reality, there was nothing strip mall about her facility. It was in a very respectable office park out past the Walmart on Route 138.

Still. Meredith didn't feel confident enough to divulge that information to Amanda the LLL Leader, or the dozen or so women assembled in the spacious living room of Amanda's Mc-Mansion. Amanda looked like a magazine ad come to life. She was absolutely symmetrical. Her make-up was flawless, and she looked incredible in her yoga pants. Meredith could have sworn she was Photoshopped. Amanda smiled at everyone and glided through the crowd of moms confidently, her Toms shoes seeming to barely touch the carpet. They milled around before the meeting proper began, snacking on flaxseed-studded corn chips and cooing over each other's babies.

Meredith had never before stepped foot in a house so big. The place was a cul-de-sac castle. She stood in a gap between the grand piano and the bookshelves, clutching her own newborn nervously. She tilted her head to the side to read the titles in the LLL Lending Library while jiggling little Stanley rhythmically. *The Womanly Art of Breastfeeding*, *Birth Without Fear*, Dr. Sears…but then something odd. A very thick old book, bound in deep red leather, with brass hinges. As Meredith began to slide the book off the shelf, its gild catching the light, one of the moms laid a hand on her shoulder.

Hell-o! My name is Gabrielle. It's so nice to see a new face!

She was a tall black woman, with perfect skinny dreadlocks and an impeccable French manicure. She had a cherub-faced toddler in a pack on her back, but she was effortlessly balanced on three inch heels.

Meredith smiled and nodded, introducing herself and Stanley.

Then Gabrielle leaned in conspiratorially, her dreads dangling, and made holy-shit-intense eye contact as she said *You know, we all came here with difficulties, Meredith. Every one of us. And now we are free. Free to love our babies, free to love ourselves.*

Gabrielle nodded with an air of profundity.

So how is Stanley's latch? she asked.

The next afternoon, she was side-lying in her bed, nursing Stanley while trying to read a McSweeney's piece on her phone. It was amusing, but her mind kept wandering to yesterday. That mom who kept humming to herself. That baby girl who Meredith could have sworn levitated for just a hot second while reaching for the vegetable-dyed handmade German wooden stacking blocks. The mom who enthusiastically insisted Meredith try sunflower oil instead of olive oil to treat Stanley's cradle cap, adding *Great things can start with a little sunflower oil. Have you ever read Bulgakov's The Master and Margarita?*

And then there were the tattoos. Somehow, perhaps by the grace of God, Meredith had managed to come of age as a young slut in the early 90s without the ubiquitous tramp stamp. But she was pretty sure all of the moms at the La Leche League meeting, many of them far younger than Meredith herself, had lower back tattoos. She'd had a chance to check them all out as the moms bent and reached while tending to their littles. There was a black cat, a lightning bolt, a gaggle of dancing skeletons. She was pretty sure a particularly weird one was supposed to be some kind of abstract giant squid.

Meredith had thanked Amanda for a helpful meeting and told her she'd be back next month, but Amanda called to follow up with her within 48 hours.

The truth is she said *we just lost one of our members. Joy. She moved to Chicago. And we were so happy to meet you. We all think you'll fit in just wonderfully with the group.*

Thanks again Meredith said.

We understand that being new in town, you might not know a lot of moms already, and we would love to offer you our support and encouragement. We want to be your best friends.

Um, OK Meredith said.

It's a commitment, Meredith. Breastfeeding is a commitment. Mothering is a commitment. Friendship is a commitment.

Wow Meredith said.

They invited her to have brunch at Charleen's house that Saturday. There were weak mimosas. And crab dip. Charleen had a slightly less intimidating house than Amanda did. She drove an older Volvo station wagon and still wore hair scrunchies. Charleen worked part-time at the Y as a Pilates instructor. She hinted that if Meredith became a LLL member, she could expect a little discount on Pilates classes too.

There's a friend code she whispered, raising her groomed eyebrows.

Meredith was wearing the same jeans she'd worn to the meeting. In fact, she hadn't washed them since then. She may or may not have slept in them one night that week too. Stanley was having trouble latching again, so she was a mess, and actually pretty glad for the brunch. She wanted Amanda to demonstrate that C-hold again, and the "breast sandwich."

Luckily, Amanda shimmied up to her right away. They moved to a quiet spot on Charleen's white leather sofa. As Meredith guided Stanley's fishfaced mouth to her exposed nipple, Amanda looked on with approval.

That's right, bring the baby to the breast, not the breast to the baby.

Meredith could feel the knotted muscles in her shoulders relaxing as Stanley settled into a rhythmic pattern of sucking and swallowing.

You see his ears move? That's when he's swallowing. He's doing well. Remember not to watch the clock. He knows how much he needs. As long as he's making plenty of wet diapers, you know he's getting enough milk.

Meredith sank back into the sofa cushions and almost cried. *It's so easy when I'm here* she said.

Suddenly, Amanda was making that creepy-as-fuck eye contact, just like the dreadlocked mom had.

It can be this easy all the time, Meredith.

A faux-hawked mom named Vanessa walked over with a half-empty mimosa flute in her hand. She was the one with the big cobra tattoo, its hood flared and its fanged mouth ready to strike. She glared at Meredith. She had iceberg blue eyes and they made Meredith shivery.

You don't have some kind of problem with witchcraft, do you? You seem like such a TOLERANT kind of person.

Meredith almost mentioned Madame Ovary then, but by some inscrutable instinct, she did not. Instead she mumbled *I went to a moon circle once before I dropped out of college. There was a cute girl named Turtle who lived in her van and we had to hold a feather and talk about our feelings.*

Amanda crinkled her brow. Vanessa rolled her cold eyes.

Look Vanessa said *We aren't some kind of pussyfoot Wiccans. Nobody's got time for that kind of shit.* She tossed back the rest of her diluted mimosa. *We're fucking metal.*

It was Meredith's turn to crinkle some part of her face. She turned to Amanda questioningly.

It's true Amanda said. *We're metal.*

Fucking metal Vanessa corrected.

Yes Amanda acquiesced. *Fucking metal.*

What's that even supposed to mean? asked Meredith.

In the simplest terms Amanda explained *we've sold our souls to the Dark Lord, Satan, for payment in abundant milk and perfectly nourished children.*

That's not really what I had in mind though said Meredith.

Look Vanessa said *we lost Joy and we need thirteen for the coven. You need to get your turds in a row and get your tattoo before the full moon.*

She was pointing her empty flute at Meredith menacingly. Her tinted lip balm was smudged.

Another mom slid onto the sofa next to Meredith and stroked Stanley's head fuzz. She was the one with the artsy squid tattoo. The one who wanted her to read Bulgakov. She wore black eyeliner and had a Sherilyn Fenn mole next to her eye.

Vanessa gets a little worked up sometimes. But it's only reasonable for us to be concerned. We have a covenant to think of. Our children are depending on us, Meredith.

Pam is right said the mom with the dancing skeleton tattoo and the two long black braids that hung over her shoulders. She passed Meredith a fresh mimosa and set a 99% post-consumer recycled paper plate of crab dip and crudités on the coffee table in front of her. *What we are talking about here is our children.*

Bijal! a mom barked from across the room. *Seriously? Eye contact much?*

Shit Bijal of the Dancing Skeleton said, picking nervously at the laces on her peasant blouse. *I forgot about the eye contact. Should I say it again?*

Oh, you don't need to said Meredith. *It seemed very sincere.*

Bijal beamed.

Thank you! That means so much. I've been doing these affirmations, you know?

OK Amanda interrupted. *Let's give Meredith a little space.*

They withdrew to beyond the edge of the coffee table. Other moms stepped forward from the reaches of the living room. They made a dense crescent of bodies around the sofa, their eyes all trained earnestly on Meredith and the baby.

I am so sure that you will think about what's best for Stanley said Amanda with a slow nod.

Babies' skulls are so soft said Vanessa.

The moms explained that Meredith wasn't really a prisoner. However, they had locked her into Charleen's master bedroom suite. She did have snacks and television and fresh guest towels stacked in the attached bath. Charleen used some kind of great fabric softener and the towels smelled really good. Meredith had never actually purchased fabric softener. She understood it in theory, though.

Meredith got Stanley down for a nap and she lay on Charleen's bed watching an episode of *Myth Busters*. She didn't have cable at home. She and Kevin were lucky to catch something interesting on PBS with the digital antenna. Meredith kind of wished she could call Kevin right then and ask him to rescue her, and she would have if the moms hadn't taken her phone, but honestly she wished even more that she could check and see if she'd won that eBay auction for the BOB Revolution Flex stroller she'd been bidding on. Kevin would likely just get pissed off at her anyway for getting herself into this mess. And she really wanted that BOB. There were so many wonderful things that she would love to have for Stanley, but she knew there was only so much that she and Kevin could afford.

If she submitted to the Great Horned Beast, Stanley would definitely have a better start in life.

On the other hand, she was pretty sure she might need her soul one day.

Meredith was loathe to risk waking Stanley, but she managed to get him fastened securely to her back with a bedsheet so she could escape out Charleen's bedroom window and go for help. She sure was glad she was wearing her stretch jeans. She had to climb down an oak tree. She cut through the back lawn that abutted Charleen's and made for the main road. The tangle of the subdivision's streets was confusing, and there were no sidewalks. Meredith started to sweat. She needed to scratch an itch under her left boob, and she was painfully aware that she would need to nurse Stanley again soon. Her armpits felt swollen.

She trudged toward yet another street named after a classical composer. A sleek black minivan glided to a stop in front of her blurry eyes. It was nigh silent. Hybrid.

Quick, get in! shouted the frizzy-haired blonde behind the wheel.

Two spit-bubbling identical redheads were rear-facing in identical Britax car seats in the middle row. This was the mom with the black cat tattoo. Maybe her name was Dinah. She had kind green eyes, love handles little enough to be adorable, and that unfortunate four-boob effect from wearing her bra a size too small. Meredith decided in one ineluctable moment that she would trust her completely.

Her name was Deirdre, not Dinah. Deirdre's house was cozy and quiet. She had a small dog with a sparkly collar. The twins crawled on the carpet and shoved plastic rings into each other's mouths. They were boys, Vern and James. Meredith nursed Stanley as she and Deirdre sat at the dining room table.

It's a fucked-up situation Deirdre started, nudging a bowl of trail mix toward her. It had dried cranberries in it, and Meredith couldn't resist, even though the thought crossed her mind that it could be poisoned or drugged. But no, just look at Deirdre. She was wearing a cute cardigan, and she had spirited her away from the group's infernal grasp.

I want out myself Deirdre continued. *I mean, I really do care about the babies. I love them. I want everything to be perfect. But devil worship is really a drag.*

I can imagine Meredith said.

Such a time suck.

I believe that.

The problem really is that I don't know if I can get my soul back now.

I guess Satan would probably be a dick about it.

Yeah.

It was one of Madame Ovary's ridiculous commercials that got Meredith thinking. The witch pranced on Deirdre's flat screen

TV in her Stevie Nicks getup, trilling in the background as Vern and James babbled at each other, poking at Stanley wrapped up like a baby burrito on the sofa. If Madame Ovary could breathe life into Meredith's shriveled uterus, wasn't it possible that she could somehow use her magic to defeat the diabolic La Leche Leaguers?

She told Deirdre her plan. They packed up the kids into Deirdre's minivan and drove toward the office park on 138. Deirdre wanted to stop in at the Walmart for a case of baby wipes and some vitamin drops, but Meredith told her to stay focused.

Madame Ovary's reception area was just as Meredith remembered it. Modern molded plastic chairs with stainless steel accents. Aloe plants and issues of *Vanity Fair*.

I was expecting wind chimes and dreamcatchers Deirdre said.

I'm telling you she's not like that at all.

Madame Ovary strode into the room in a tasteful beige pantsuit.

Meredith! How wonderful to see you again. Oh, and the baby! How sweet he is.

Stanley gurgled.

We need your help Meredith said. *Our souls are in peril.*

Please Madame Ovary said *step into my exam room.*

Madame Ovary introduced herself briskly to Deirdre, handing her a crisp card embossed with her name and website. She wasted no time in getting down to business. The La Leche League moms had been on Madame Ovary's radar. In fact, she knew quite a bit about them. Amanda's pregnancy, and her darling daughter Echo, were the results of Madame Ovary's magic. Madame O revealed that it hadn't been until after Amanda's successful orgasmic dolphin water birth, when she realized that her inverted nipples would be a hurdle, that she turned to the dark side. Amanda had cursed her nipples and cursed God. She'd punched herself in the head and wept bitterly into her fenugreek tea.

Her grief was too much to bear Madame Ovary said. *She was like a woman possessed.*

Because she was possessed? Meredith asked.

Well, yes Madame Ovary replied. *And I fought for her, I did. I was able to cast a protective circle around her for a short time. But in the end, my Grand Caravan is just such a piece-a-shit.*

Excuse me? Deirdre said.

My minivan. The only way you're going to be able to win your soul from Satan is drag racing. It's kind of his thing.

Drag racing? Meredith asked.

He calls it Minivan Mayhem.

Amanda stood in the middle of the cul-de-sac, her house looming behind her, flanked by all the moms with their babies strapped to their bodies in various contortions. She wore Echo in a high back carry, crisscrossed by a woven wrap of turquoises and pinks. Her lips curled into a glossy snarl.

Madame Ovary, we meet again.

Yes, but this time you aren't blubbering 'Breast Is Best' hysterically while rolling in the gutter.

Amanda tossed her Pantene-commercial hair and bounced on the balls of her feet to keep Echo babbling happily.

Things have changed.

Vanessa stepped out of the crowd. *Enough bullshit* she said. *Let's do this.*

Yes Madame Ovary agreed. *Where's your Prince of Darkness?*

Vanessa grimaced tetchily. *That's just passive aggressive, O. You know he prefers* Prince of Light.

Darkness is really more apt though, isn't it?

Lucifer Vanessa snapped. *LUCIFER, Prince of LIGHT.*

Whatever Madame Ovary said.

So where is he? Meredith asked.

A voice boomed out across the cul-de-sac. HERE I AM.

Satan sounded remarkably like Bill Cosby doing Fat Albert. Meredith turned to see that he did not look like Fat Albert or even Bill Cosby at all. He looked middle-aged and Caucasian, unexceptional save for the hooves and the jean jacket with Chinese dragons painted on the sleeves.

Does he always talk like that? Meredith asked.

Like what? Amanda said.

You know, the Fat Albert thing.

Oh-em-gee Bijal piped up, her braids swinging. *Are you seriously fat-shaming him? And I bet you call yourself a feminist.* Bijal still had baby weight. Her dancing skeletons were a little stretched.

No, the cartoon Meredith said. *Jesus, I really am the Old Mom, aren't I?*

Uh-uh-uh Amanda said, wagging a finger. *Legally, we can't use the J-word. There was a whole packet of paperwork. The J-Man doesn't want to have anything to do with Minivan Mayhem.*

A fucking square, if you ask me said Vanessa.

Satan snickered.

Then he snarled at Meredith IT'S NOT FAT ALBERT, IT'S GLENN DANZIG, YOU BITCH.

Do you EVER use your Inside Voice? Bijal grumbled. The squirming lump in her ring sling whimpered every time The Dark Lord spoke.

WE'RE NOT EVEN INSIDE, BIJAL.

Still. Bijal pursed her lips.

NOT EVEN INSIDE.

Still.

OK, enough already Deirdre said. *What are you driving? We're using my minivan.*

Ooooh! The hybrid! Pam gasped. Her mole wiggled as her eyes widened.

Satan shook his head and snorted. *TREE-HUGGERS.*

The Prince of LIGHT will be driving my 2016 Lexus IS Vanessa said. *Suck on that and choke.*

Meredith sat on the curb nursing Stanley while the moms programmed their GPS units and loaded the babies into their car seats. Fussing toddlers were demanding yogurt tubes and nut-free granola bars. Now that Satan and Bijal were done bickering, they were making out. He was pressing her against the hood of Charleen's clapped-out Volvo, his long nails pawing eagerly at the prodigious curves beneath her pink yoga pants. Bijal giggled. Meredith tried not to stare. Amanda walked over to Meredith and looked at Stanley with soft eyes.

How is he feeding now? she asked. *Better?*

Meredith nodded.

He really is a cutie Amanda offered.

Look Amanda Meredith said *I know you're not a total twat.*

Thanks Amanda said. *I meant it when I said we liked you.*

The thing is, inverted nipples aren't the end of the world. As a La Leche League Leader, you should know that.

Amanda was obviously taken aback. Her eyebrows bobbed.

Yeah said Meredith. *Sorry, but Madame Ovary told us all about your boob fail.*

You don't know what it was like Amanda whispered.

I know what it's like to be exhausted and trying and wearing the same jeans for a week straight.

Amanda attempted a polite smile, but it wobbled on her face.

You've never worn dirty pants for a week, have you?

No said Amanda.

The point is, you can do this. It might be hard sometimes without the witchcraft, but just like you said, breastfeeding is a commitment. We'll all have each other for support. Isn't that what La Leche League is all about?

Amanda's eyes were humid.

But I couldn't even get pregnant without Madame Ovary.

Me either! But here we are Meredith said. She stood up and laid some of that insane eye contact on Amanda. *We are going to win this race. We are going to win back the souls of the whole coven. Being a mom is hard, but you can do it without Satan's help.*

I just don't know said Amanda.

They met on a long straight stretch of Route 138. The moon was full and the rivets on Satan's jean jacket gleamed. Parked minivans lined both sides of the asphalt. The coven moms drank smoothies that they had picked up on the way, and Meredith kicked herself for not thinking of it herself. She considered asking one of them for a juice box or something. Madame Ovary was pulling on leather driving gloves. She'd shed her beige office attire in favor of a bright red zippered jumpsuit, also leather.

She could totally pull off wearing a mask with that Deirdre said from over Meredith's shoulder.

Meredith nodded. *Very superhero. She is so hot.*

OK BITCHES Satan announced. *IT'S TIME TO ROLL.*

Let me just remind you all Amanda said *that we're racing for SOULS.*

Her look lingered on Meredith.

And for the children! Pam exclaimed.

Vanessa shoved past Pam and stood inches from Meredith's face. *You could have been cooperative* she said. *You could have been a HELPER.*

I just really want to keep my soul though Meredith said.

Vanessa's nostrils twitched. *Because you're LAME SAUCE.*

The engines of the two minivans roared. The moms cheered. Lightning bisected the starry sky, and everybody turned to look at Satan in Vanessa's Lexus.

YEAH he said. *I DID THAT.*

Meredith hustled over to Deirdre's minivan and stuck her head into the open driver's side window.

Thank you, Madame O. Thank you so much for doing this.

Madame Ovary's gloved hand shot out and grabbed a fistful of Meredith's t-shirt.

YOU'VE got to do this, Meredith.

What? Fuck that!

No, seriously Madame Ovary said. *The Dark Lord has defeated me once already. You have to take the wheel. It's the only way we can save their souls.*

Meredith balked. *You're just having a little dip in confidence, that's all.*

No, no. I'm really great at fertility magic but I'm shit at drag racing.

Well, FUCK said Meredith. *Let me get Stanley in the car seat.*

Meredith was no expert on the unwritten social contract normal people have about the rules of drag racing, but she was certain Satan was driving dirty. He was *not* keeping in his lane. And just seconds after they'd both done their wicked burnouts, a thick swarm of demons had erupted from the side window of Satan's minivan and covered the windshield of Meredith's. They looked like Jim Henson goblins, and she tried to knock them loose with the wipers. It only helped a little. They slobbered on the glass, and Meredith peered between them as she buried the needle of the speedometer. The soundtrack from the *Curious George* movie blared through the speakers.

Jack Johnson, give me strength.

The Lexus swerved and nudged Meredith's bumper. She skidded into the gravel shoulder and back onto the asphalt. They were fast approaching the bend before the Walmart parking lot, where they'd agreed to turn back. The layer of demons on the windshield burst into flames. Suddenly, the cab of the minivan was ripe with the tangy yeast smell of breastmilk poop.

Oh damn Meredith said. She pressed the button for the hazard lights and eased onto the shoulder.

She was crouched in the backseat holding Stanley's ankles in one hand and gently swabbing his tush with a baby wipe when Satan sauntered up to the minivan and leaned into the open sliding side door.

WHATCHA DOIN'? he asked.

What's it look like? Meredith replied. *Stanley made poops.*

Satan nodded and dragged one hoof through the gravel casually.

OH, I LIKE THIS SONG he said, jutting his chin toward the stereo.

Meredith snapped the harness over Stanley's chest. She really didn't want to make small talk.

I WAS THINKING MAYBE WE COULD, LIKE, HANG OUT AND JUST SEE HOW WE GET ALONG.

No, thanks Meredith said. *Let's just finish with the drag racing thing.*

Satan grimaced. YOU KNOW, I'M KIND OF MISUNDERSTOOD.

OK then Meredith said, shrugging. *Do you want to forfeit?*

NO he said petulantly. BUT WE COULD MAKE A DEAL WHERE I JUST EAT THE BABY AND WE CALL IT EVEN.

You're an asshole.

Meredith slid back into the driver's seat.

NO, I'M REALLY NOT Satan said. WHAT ABOUT IF WE JUST GO BACK TO MY RAPE CAVE AND WATCH SOME NETFLIX?

Meredith slammed the door shut and revved the engine.

Rape jokes are never funny.

She pounded her foot on the accelerator and peeled out, sending a spray of gravel into the Dark Lord's face as she turned. He hissed and hid his visage behind one side of his jean jacket.

Smoldering demons slid from the windshield and scattered in a cloud of ash. Meredith hauled ass.

She was half way back to the moms when she saw him in the rearview mirror, hell-bent on overtaking her, the Lexus a flaming streak on the center line. The night sky roiled above him, curdling with masses of black clouds and stabbed by lightning. Thunder shook the road and the asphalt cracked just yards ahead of Meredith. She slammed on the brakes as hard as she could, and the minivan spun sideways, airbags deploying.

Meredith clawed her way out of the driver's seat and tumbled toward Stanley. He was blinking and sucking contentedly, his three middle fingers jammed between his pink lips. Meredith unfastened his five-point harness and scooped him into her arms. Satan's minivan was screeching to a halt beside the wreckage of her own.

He stood in the middle of the road, his bland Caucasian forehead now bulging with curling ram's horns. He unfurled a gigantic pair of midnight blue wings, the feathers crackling with electricity. His pants were now missing, and his terrifyingly huge penis was erect and barbed. When he bellowed, Meredith realized that she had never before heard a true bellow. She felt like her kneecaps would split open.

But she ran.

She clutched Stanley tightly and ran like the fucking wind. She would finish the race on foot and win those souls if it killed her. Satan chased after, his wings still spread wide, his hooves sending up sparks and cracking the asphalt with each impact. Meredith could see the moms in the distance, lining the sides of the road. They were stomping and cheering. One of the toddler moms waved a Baby Bjorn potty in the air above her head, like a drunk chick at a Skynyrd concert waving her bra. Meredith wasn't sure who they were actually rooting for at this point, but it didn't matter. She just ran as fast as she could. She thought that if it were a movie, it would be the perfect time for a flashback to reveal she'd been a high school track star. Unfortunately, as a girl Meredith just hung out behind the bleachers and smoked pot. Satan was literally breathing down her neck.

She was millimeters away from feeling his talons sink deep into the meat of her shoulders when Amanda came screaming out of the underbrush like a wild and glorious yoga-pantsed banshee, tackling Satan with her full body weight and ramming her bent elbow straight into his windpipe. He flew off his hooves sideways, his great thorny member swinging helplessly as he gasped for air. He hit the road and the ground shook. Meredith felt a surge of adrenalin as she turned and sprinted toward the finish.

She collapsed into mom arms, hyperventilating. Madame Ovary cradled Stanley as Meredith's head swayed on her neck and her eyes rolled madly. Pam clamped a paper Trader Joe's grocery sack over her mouth and instructed her to breathe deeply.

Unholy fuck, you actually did it Vanessa said. She stood there slack-jawed, unsure what to do next. There was nobody she needed to threaten.

We're free! Deirdre squealed.

Moms were looking at each other in confusion, clutching their babies anxiously.

What's going to happen now? Pam asked, her black-lined eyes gone big again.

She removed the bag from Meredith's face, and Meredith tried to answer, but her lips were rubber and her vision dissolved.

I am SO happy you could make it Meredith said, opening her front door wide. *Everybody else is already here!*

She'd put up a decorative wreath for the occasion. A thick circle of braided ivy speckled with spray glitter hung on the painted yellow wood.

Amanda stood on Meredith's doorstep beaming, Echo in an Ergo on her back. The classic, discontinued insect print. It must have cost her a small fortune.

She hugged Meredith warmly.

You know I wouldn't miss it for the world! It's not just any day a Leader hosts her first La Leche League meeting!

I owe it all to you, Amanda.

Oh, stop. She blushed.

Then she leaned in and did the eye contact.

It's a commitment Amanda said. *Breastfeeding, mothering. Friendship.*

Meredith smiled and lifted up the back of her t-shirt to show her new tattoo.

What do you think?

Oh! said Amanda. *Oh. My. God. A flaming minivan. That is SO you.*

Bird was gone

It was some kind of turbulence, a shiver in the air. A disturbance, like a heat wave rising off of blacktop on a scorching day, except it was cold then, brutally cold. Bird was wearing his little green parka over his requisite fleecy dinosaur jammies, and a thick red wool cap over his long wisps of white-blonde hair. Blue mittens. Winter could not be allowed to disrupt his routine. His pajamas, his buttered penne pasta for lunch, his time in the sandbox after, pushing his feet through the sand for twenty minutes. And then his hide time. He ducked into the wardrobe side of the dresser, and Becca watched him shut the door behind him, as she had a hundred times before. But then the tremor, and her heart dropped. She flew from the back steps, across the yard toward the sandbox, fell to her knees in front of the dresser, the mud under the dead grass soaking through her jeans. Something was wrong, she knew. She wrenched open the small white door and saw that Bird was gone.

Becca and her husband Sam had bought the dresser at a flea market one Saturday afternoon when they were still just dating.

Back when she was just a pretty single mom with a shitty waitressing job and Sam didn't fully grasp how other-than-normal Bird was. Sam wanted to refinish the child-size chest of drawers, scrape off the old white paint, line it with colorful contact paper. He was excited about the project. He set it out by the fence in the backyard of his house, next to the sandbox he'd installed for Bird, planning on doing the work out there. But Bird had taken to it as it was, where it was. He liked to hide inside. By the time Becca and Bird had moved into Sam's house, it couldn't be moved, couldn't be changed. When things were good for Bird, it was best to keep them good. The dresser had got weathered, warped. But so had Sam's patience. At first, it was okay, the strange kid, James, called Bird because of the way he flapped his arms. But Sam started to push, insist that Bird try new clothes, new foods. Bird would throw himself to the ground, bang his head against the floor or the dirt. His mouth would open wide in a simulacrum of terror although no sound emerged and his eyes did not register fear. Sam used words like indulgence and spoil. Sam threatened to take his axe to the dresser. At five, Bird was still nonverbal. At five, Bird still couldn't stand to be touched.

And now, Bird was gone.

Becca dropped back onto her bottom, felt the damp creep through to her skin. She saw him go in, she saw him. She'd been watching. Some days, when the weather was warmer, she'd let him play for a while unobserved, busy herself in the kitchen and leave the back door open. Check every few minutes. There was a privacy fence, and the gate was heavy. It wasn't like he could wander off. But she'd been watching the whole time that day. She'd been sitting on the back steps, huddled in her down coat, her hands plunged deep into the pockets, watching every move he'd made under the winter-naked maple tree as the wind rubbed her cheeks raw. Sam didn't like it when Bird was left to himself at all.

Sam said he didn't trust Bird not to drown himself in a teaspoon of puddle water. Sam thought it was *negligent* for her to leave Bird to watch cartoons while she took a shower. Becca's lungs heaved with panic. Her phone was in her pocket, but she couldn't call Sam. She couldn't call the police. It just didn't make any sense. Maybe she'd cracked. Her neck whipped around, she screamed *Bird!* But she knew he wasn't there. Becca slammed the little white door shut and rested her forehead against it repeating *Please please please.*

Then it sprang open, and Bird tumbled into her arms. Becca clutched him tightly on instinct, but caught herself and jerked away, sure that he would, as usual, fight her unbearable embrace. But he didn't. He flung his arms around her neck and bleated into her wind-tangled hair *Ma*. Becca trembled, tears streaming, as she scooped him up and ran into the house. He touched her. He spoke. Unbelievable. It wasn't until she slumped onto the kitchen linoleum with Bird rocking safely in her arms that she noticed he was wearing different clothes. Baggy rough-spun pants, some kind of hairy thick sweater. He was barefoot, his little boots gone. *My God* she said *Where did you go?* She pulled back from him, tried to assess him objectively. She was sure he'd grown taller, his hair longer. *And how long have you been gone?*

It was a long-ago-long-ago dream thrumming up from the deep. When Becca was a child, she'd been like any other kid who chased rabbits from between the rows of their Granny's garden plot, hoping to find the bottomless burrow that would lead to Wonderland. She'd leaped from the crest of the cellar steps and landed as a pile of bruised bones after clapping her hands with fierce faith and proclaiming her belief in faerie. She'd searched for Borrowers in every cranny of her home. When her Aunt Ramona married a fobby Irishman with a thick brogue, she'd scoured every inch of his musty house, sure she would find Wee Folk nested behind the furniture, or *bean sidhe* in the attic. She'd tried to disappear into sidewalk chalk paintings, and on every dark and stormy night she awaited the arrival of mysterious and magical vagabonds swathed in stolen sheets. But Becca's greatest obsession, by far, was her quest to find a passage to Narnia. She pushed her way through the coats at the back of her mother's closet dozens of times, rubbing her cheeks against the soft suede and furry trim, desperate in her desire for them to turn into fir boughs in the snow. She prepared herself mentally, year after year, for the happy eventuality of finding entry to enchantment, of fleeing the real world with its multiplication tables and doctor's needles and Brussels sprouts. Like every other kid searching for the fabled escape hatch, never in all that time had she really considered what it would have been like for her parents if she had succeeded.

Becca watched Bird as he slept, watched his eyes jittering, sealed safely under their lids. She touched the palm of his relaxed hand with one easy fingertip, brushed a pale wing of hair from his uncreased forehead. Sometimes she sat for hours in the rocking chair, in the pool of night-light, watching his sleek belly rise and fall with the steady rhythm of his breath. She rocked to the rhythm, they moved together, they danced. Together.

His own little world. That's what people liked to say.

She'd folded the strange clothes and secreted them away on a closet shelf.

Becca stood at Bird's bedroom window and looked out into the dark backyard. The white of the dresser was like the moon. She knew that she would not war against its gravity.

Bird hid every day, and winter opened its cold fist. Green nudged up through the garden soil. Becca knelt and dug with her trowel as Bird plowed his feet through the sandbox and shut himself behind the wooden door of the dresser. It was on a sunny afternoon in May that he started listening to the roots. Becca was transplanting day lilies, and a clump of them was laid out on damp sheets of newspaper as she carefully divided the rhizome. Bird crept up and pressed his ear to its flesh. Becca wiped her muddy hands on her thighs and watched as he cradled a plant in his skinny arms, carried it to the dresser and shut it inside.

After that first incident, he'd come into the garden often, kneeling down to the dirt, listening at the roots of various flowers or herbs. Sometimes he would wander away without disturbing the soil, but frequently he would pluck a plant whole, gently trying to do no damage to its roots, and ferry it to the wardrobe. Lemon balm, Shasta daisies, spearmint, Holy basil.

They all disappeared.

One minute, two. Ten. Thirty. The sweat stains on Becca's yellow tank top spread out from under her arms, down her back. The small stray curls from her ponytail clung damply to her neck. She paced the backyard like a caged tiger. *Please please please.* It was the only prayer she knew. The midday sun was high and hot, the garden soil parched. She rinsed her hands under the outdoor spigot, worked the mud from under her fingernails, sat on the back steps with nervously jerking knees.

One hour, two. She flew down the basement stairs, into the cool darkness, and reemerged with the hidden pack of cigarettes that Sam stashed in the bottom drawer of his toolbox. She lit one after the other, striking wooden kitchen matches and tossing them spent into the holly bushes that flanked the back door. She crushed the butts into an empty can fished from the recycling bin. Her eyes were swollen, overflowing, and between fierce drags of smoke she bit her bottom lip, drew blood.

She beat on the little door. She tried to crawl inside, fold her impossibly adult body into the tight hallowed space. She lay on her back with her face to the sky, all of the whispering roots beneath her keeping their secrets, and she sobbed.

Three hours. Bird was gone just over three hours. He returned again in strange clothes, with longer hair. A well-healed scar ran the length from his shoulder to his elbow. His cheeks were rosy apples, and he looked her in the eye. Bird smiled.

Eye contact. Smiling. These things had never happened before. Maybe they wouldn't happen again. After all, Bird had never repeated that *Ma*. He'd never again reached out to touch her, or let her clutch him close without a struggle. And yet.

Becca cradled him like a baby, carried him upstairs to the bathtub as he bucked in her arms. Already he was withdrawing from her. She stripped him of the anachronistic clothes, sat him on the edge of the toilet seat as she opened the taps. The scar shined pinkly, and his feet were caked with mud that shimmered as if it were laced with gold dust. Becca knelt before Bird on the bathmat and pinched a tiny morsel of dirt from the crust on his left foot. It crumbled between her fingers, glimmering, and she touched it with her tongue softly. It tasted of cinnamon, and something else. Something almost familiar, but not.

Warm bath water closed around Bird's body, and swirled with trails of the sparkling mud. Becca watched his reflection in the chrome of the spigot, a small Bird flapping his wings, slapping his hands against the surface. Droplets landed on her face and she felt too tired to wipe them away. The scar was long, and the cut must have been deep. He'd been hurt, certainly, but he'd also been cared for, mended. Somebody had cleaned his wound, stitched it shut, tended to it.

And he'd come home with a smile. A grin of motley big-and-little teeth, lips curving and splitting apart like a ripe fruit. Sparks of recognition in his eyes like never before. Becca could have taken Sam's axe to the cabinet right then, she could have ended it. But she couldn't bring herself to do it. She looked at her own face in the bathroom mirror, her eyes wreathed with broken blood vessels, her hair disheveled and nose sunburned. She knew she was scared more for herself than for Bird. Wherever it was that he was going, it was a magical place. A place where he was helped, guarded. A place where those plants had wanted to go. Maybe, it was a world where he could be Bird in a way that he could not be here. A Bird who knew laughter, words, connection. Becca wanted so much to have that Bird for herself. But she knew even then that that Bird would never be hers. Becca got down on her knees, cried as she fought the flurry of his blows to wash his hair and wrap him in his towel. He arched his back away from her as she carried him to his bed. His small fists banged against her ears and his heels dug into her ribs as she wrangled him into his pajamas. Bird finally broke free of her grasp, and rocked himself to sleep as she sat and watched, as always.

He'd started carrying a purple rubber snake with him. He'd kept it with him always, stroking its long body, slinging it over his shoulder when he busied himself with another task. It was an overcast autumn afternoon and she'd run inside to switch the laundry from the washer to the dryer. She looked out the window and saw the snake abandoned in the grass in front of the dresser. She knew. Bird was gone. Somehow, she knew Bird was gone for good.

Hours passed. Sam came home from work and found Becca sitting in Bird's room alone in the dark. She'd finished crying. She rocked in the rocking chair, remembering how they'd moved in rhythm, danced. How they'd done that, together.

There were flyers all over the neighborhood. Pleas for help on the television and radio. Internet alerts. Questions from the police, questions repeated. Becca had nothing to tell but the truth. So, the suspicion. The house turned upside down, the search for evidence, the yellow tape. The hospital. The pills. The electricity. Sam's goodbye, his eyes pinched and his voice serrated. The divorce papers. Becca smiled gently and said *Sam, you know I never loved you*. He put his fist through the wall of the hospital rec room.

The little apartment of her own, quiet and hollow. She called and asked Sam for the dresser, and he told her what she had already guessed. The dresser had been destroyed. Sam had hacked it to pieces, burned it in the backyard while the neighbors rubbernecked and called the cops and Channel Eleven on their cell phones. Sam's new wife croaked in the background *Hang up, baby* and the dial tone buzzed in her ear.

She hadn't thought Bird would return through the little white door, but she'd hoped maybe she would be able to send him something. She didn't have a garden anymore, but she grew herbs on all the windowsills of her apartment, and on the fire escape. She pressed her ear to the terra cotta pots, listened for some murmur. She heard nothing, but sometimes she would unearth a plant, roots and all, and leave it as an offering in the back of her closet. She would trail her fingers along the dresses and coats, press her palms to the wall and wish it would open to let her in, whispering *Please please please*. It was the only prayer she knew.

The female of the species

I was born with a full set of teeth. Before I first opened my eyes, I drew my tongue across the ridges of bone that filled my mouth. I never knew a mother's breast. I heard the sounds of the night: the husking of wings in the air above me, the murmuring of deep roots braiding themselves into black soil below, the witching music of millions of insects gifting me with my name: *Leeleet, Leeleet, Leeleet.* I knew I was alone in the Garden but for my Maker; the Maker who moved through all things, the invisible made visible, speaking to me through all sounds, all mouths and all song.

I heard the sounds of the night, and I opened my eyes.

The moon was whole and it was my heart, white and bright. I did not know then that it was made only to be a mirror for the sun, that it reflected the light of a greater creation. I saw it, burning and pure, and I felt its true home behind my ribs ache and reach, craving. The moon dragged me forward and upward, magnetized the hollow in my chest, led me into the swarm of life that coalesced around my body, the sweet center of the universe.

I swam through the rich night air, danced through the Garden, limbs unhindered, with its light washing over my dark skin, slipping between the strands of my black hair.

Its light crowned me.

Rabbits rustled in the underbrush, darted through the silvered fields, and I could hear their blood roar. I watched mesmerized, my hands stilled, as a wolf bounded after and caught one, crushed its throat in lusty jaws. The thirsty earth sighed, grateful. The dreaming grasses trembled. The wolf's desire thundered, and I felt it course through me and flood my belly. I understood the hunger the Maker had given us, its elegance.

I wept for joy.

Tears smelled like the sea; I remembered then the Maker drawing my substance from the ocean floor, carrying the mud up from the deeps, shaping me and breathing the wind into my virgin lungs. I licked my lips and tasted the salt there, still clinging. I put my hands to my breasts, my belly, my hips, and felt the perfection of the Maker's work. I smoothed the soft hair under my arms, between and on my legs. I wiggled my toes and laughed.

The first laugh.

I raced after the wolf, running between the trees heavy with fruit, my feet a blur beneath me. The strength in my legs was hot and rapturous, and I ripped through the shadows. The world was dark and lush. It was abundant and new. And I believed then that it had been made for me.

Dawn began to blanch the sky.

I sat under a pomegranate tree and tore into a fruit, splitting its rind and digging out the pulpy seeds. I ate, the juice staining my hands and mouth red. The sun blistered the sky, its brightness scouring everything. The night sounds faded and new creatures emerged. Deer ambled on skinny legs through the morning dew, bright birds chattered in the treetops, lizards darted into puddles of sunlight. Honeybees thrummed. And then I saw him, backlit by the scorching orb, for a moment limned by its burn, the silhouette of a figure like mine and yet so different. He walked toward me and his face became clear, shrouded in dark curls, his beard wild and the hair of his head spilling over his shoulders. His black eyes pierced me. Adam.

I looked upon him, and I loved him.

His skin was spiced with the taste of dirt. He had been made from the dry earth, from the red clay. He kissed my mouth and tangled his hands in my hair. His breath was hot and rapid. We sank into the grass, we tumbled. He tried to pin me beneath him, but I rolled again and again, finally easing him into my body as I gazed down at his face. I saw something flash in his eyes then. It was hard and angry, but it melted away as I rocked against him. His mouth went slack.

His seed smoldered in me.

I sat beside him, stroking his legs as the wind bent the heads of the wildflowers around us. I traced his hipbone with my toes. I smiled and laughed *I want more*. It was a moment of jagged edge and brutality as he said my name for the first time. It was so different on his lips than it had been when the insects exalted me. I understood then its meaning. *Night-demon*.

Adam named all things, and I was first among them.

He knocked me back onto the earth, held me down with his arms. There was growling in his throat, the bridled strain of thunder. I struggled and he tore at my hair. He thrust himself inside. He bent his head close to my ear and said my name again. I bit into his neck. I ripped his flesh with my teeth.

The taste of his blood was fathomless.

I ran. I left him to his Maker, and I ran, the sunlight blinding me. I was hounded by unseen beasts. There were birds shrieking and diving to pierce my skin, until I plunged into the forest that skirted the Garden. I ran until I was shaded, and then I lay panting on the moss among silent stones. My head throbbed, my feet were battered. I was braceleted with bruises, and his blood was still on my tongue.

    I shivered and knew I could never return.

The cave walls wept. I thought that the earth itself was shedding tears for me. The sea was near; the scent of salt was heavy on the air, heavy enough to taste. I had wandered, moving like a black clot of shadow through the nights, deeper into the wilderness. Food was not easy to find beyond the bounds, but when I reached the shore I feasted. I collected seaweeds, and caught the crawling crabs. I cracked them open with my teeth and sucked the meat from their shells. I snatched up the fish that were abandoned by the tides in rocky pools, and bit into their moony bellies. Tiny iridescent scales clung to my fingers. I swallowed their eyes whole and I saw what they saw, coldness and deepness and the blackness of water forever shifting and teeming.

    I ate and I saw.

    The Maker called for my return. The shrieks of the gulls chastised me, the winds rose and pushed me back, but I refused. I heard the waves at dawn as I curled for sleep in the shelter of the cave, I heard the Maker's voice in the thunder of the sea and the moaning of the rocks, but I turned my face to the weeping walls and hardened my heart. I remembered Adam's eyes and I felt the bindings between us tighten and pull, but I pulled back. I heard the sound of roots being torn from the soil.

    I dreamed only of the watery dark.

    When I felt the quickening in my womb, the Messengers arrived. They were three, with faces like Adam's but for the light. Light unspooling from every pore, singeing my eyelashes. I averted my gaze and they moved in my periphery like birds, quick and sharp. *Fear not* they said, but I did. They carried the Maker's command. Flushed and sweating, I fell to my knees. I cowered on the floor of the cave and scratched at my eyes, howling. Hatred bloomed in my breast, burst into black flower with the spice of decay. They told me that I carried Adam's children in my body, that they would belong to Adam and his Maker. *His Maker.* I lashed out at the tallest of the Messengers. I grabbed for his throat, I spat and gnashed my teeth.

And he placed a hand on my belly.

I felt my womb churn. Blood striped my legs. I crawled deeper into the cave, and tried to hide in the fissures of the wet rock, but the Messengers walked after me, slowly. They watched by the light of themselves as dark bodies emerged from mine. Hundreds. Twisted, scaled and feathered. Hundreds, with pleading eyes and spiked mouths. They poured from me and they swarmed back, tumbling over one another wailing. They scraped and snapped as they fought to latch at my breasts.

I had no milk for these, my demon children.

My children devoured me. My tears were bitter but I knew that they had to be fed. They tore me to pieces and sucked the marrow from my splintered bones. They grappled, their claws bright, their beaks and scales splashed with my blood, fighting each other for my heart. The Messengers watched. At this time, the Maker had not yet given the gift of death to humans. I did not die. Something of me swelled and teemed inside of my children's wretched bodies. They circled the Messengers, gliding around them in the cave's fetid air, and I watched from their eyes, I felt their hunger. The one who laid hand on my belly reached out and caught a lashing tail.

The Messenger began to rebuild me.

With threads of light he sewed me from their bodies, discarding some pieces that fell to ash, reshaping others to fit my new form. He sang as he remade me, and the music of it, the meaning of it, this song of praise, was unbearable to me. I itched. I knew agony. The other Messengers joined their voices to his and my body expanded to match the vastness of the skies. The pain too grew to fit me. Thunder pitched me, screeching, into a fathomless black.

Then all was silent, my body small again on the earth.

I moved my fingers first. They were tipped with claws. I felt my breasts, my belly. These parts of me were like the human woman I was, but covered in the pelt of a beast. From my back sprouted two wings. My mouth was fanged. My legs were scaled, gleaming white, and ended with the talons of an owl. I crouched, and the long hair of my head, now pale and thin, spread over my shoulders like cobweb. I could see into the dark, I could see for miles. I could see Adam, and I could smell him.

I could feel his heartbeat disturbing the air between us.

I desired him. I thought the thirst would kill me. And I could see his new wife beside him, underneath him. Her arms were soft and her voice was sweet. *Chava.* Chava whispered to him like wild honey, and was made of his flesh. I could smell her too, the scent of ripest fruit bursting its rind. She walked beside Adam, a pet, and he touched her tenderly. I crouched in my cold cave by the sea, remade as a monster, and Chava danced in the sun, her skin golden. She kissed Adam's neck and fed him berries from her hand. Her belly swelled and she woke from napping in the long grasses with laughter flowering from her lips.

I had laughed once, too.

I began to go to him as he slept. The night was my veil. I tore through the starry sky and came to him with my mouth open, my wings wide. I burrowed into his dreams. Adam dreamed of the vast sea, of stone towers, and glittering fields of snow. He dreamed of things he'd never seen. I wormed into those visions.

I twisted myself into the colors, and sang from behind his own breathing. I grasped his flesh, my hands caked with blood. He moaned beneath me, arcing his spine. In the dark, he remembered my name.

His seed was pearls in my fist.

I took from him and I birthed again and again, flooding the world with my children. Their features were mangled, their bellies distended with wrath. They were monsters, marked by hoof and horn, claw and fang. Their eyes danced with hunger. They seethed. They scrabbled across the land, dredged the waters. They smelled of decay. They bristled with malice, and occupied the wastes.

They made ruin everywhere they swarmed.

And I returned to Adam time after time. He knew that it was I who stroked him in the blind night. He slept apart from Chava, ashamed. He looked away from her eyes, cringed at her touch. There was distance dilating between them, and she cried into her bed of petals and feathers. She did not know what festered in the shadows and pulled him away. She thirsted for the knowledge. She suffered and distrusted the Maker.

She went to the Tree for answers.

And I, on my belly, told her she would know. My tongue flickered in her ear. I whispered, twining myself around her soft arms. I hissed and hummed with pleasing words. I spoke of love. I spoke of fate. I offered her the fig, full of wasps. Chava reached out her hand and cupped the fruit in her palm. Her eyes shined with dumb hope. She bit through its skin and into its flesh. *Go* I said *and share with your husband. This will bind him to you forever.*

They did weep, together.

I lit upon the fiery Sword and watched them go. They were huddled in pelts, their tears trailing behind them like shining pebbles. Beyond the borders, they knew the cold that had bitten my bones. And they knew the fear of death that I would never know. Adam struck the earth again and again, pleading for food. He scythed and sweated. Soil blackened his fingernails and his hands hardened. Chava squatted in the rushes and expelled her whelps in spasms of agony. She begged the Maker for mercy and received none. She buried the placentas to hide them from the wolves, but the beasts uncovered them and gorged on her children's blood before her eyes. Her babies were toothless and unfinished, weak and puny. The first were Kayin and Hevel.

 I knew them both so well.

Kayin and Hevel both had the eyes of their father, and I watched them grow. As Adam silvered and his belly sagged, they looked more like Adam than he himself did. They grew tall and strong and they ripened. Their blood pulsed hot and they began to dream of wives, turning in their beds. That is when I came to them, rustling in the moonless dark of their tent. I slithered between their bodies. I bit and sucked and spread my wings over their limbs. Hevel smelled of goats, of blood and skins, and Kayin smelled always of the earth, of clay and verdant things.

 They reached for me in the night, their hands hungry for more.

 Hevel had the hands of his mother, slender fingers and gentle touch. Kayin had the hands of Adam, hard and thewy, knuckles beaded with scabs. Hevel tended his flock with poemy devotion, and wept for the weak among them. Kayin blistered with lust for his work; it was the struggle that he loved. He licked the sweat from the hair of his lip and plowed possessed. He saw the earth swallow all that lived and he made war to steal life back from it. Hevel was honeycomb in my mouth, but Kayin was fire.

 It was Kayin I loved.

He began to seek me in the night, roaming into the fields. He listened for the thresh of my wings. He watched for my eyes in the darkness between the stalks of grain, and called my name when he heard the cries of the owls. He wished to keep me from his brother. His rancor started as a tight seed in his belly, but it soon cracked wide. His enmity unfurled and flourished. He burned bright. His face shined with raw light when he caught me by my wrists and pinned me to the dirt. For Kayin, I let it be done. For Kayin, I would have given anything.

But my hunger was not mine to give.

I still bit into Hevel, I still hovered over him as he writhed in his blankets. I stole his seed as often as Kayin's and I birthed his babies as well as his brother's, though they were as twisted and frightening as the ones that had come before. The brothers never saw their hooved sons, never held their serpentine daughters. My children did not resemble their fathers at all, and they always left me. The daughters of Chava were beautiful and they cooed at her breast. They grew like willows with indomitable roots and bore their own golden babies. My babies flew, they ran scuttling into the seething darkness. They disappeared into the wastes, into the gray and uneasy seas. When I tried to cling to them they screeched and ripped hair loose from my head, trampled it into the mud of my cave. My scalp showed through in patches. Scars scored my flesh. I became more hideous to look upon.

I snatched instead at the golden babies, and I strangled.

Every woman has the instinct to silence a crying baby. Most will soothe, pat and whisper, cradle the child's supple flesh in obliging arms. Guide the open mouth to the nipple. Hold the baby safe and tight. But some will hold tighter than others. Some will be more desperate for abeyance. Some will turn to knuckle or knife; some women will summon death itself to buy respite. Millennia have wended their way past my cave, bringing with them every mother. I have seen them all. I have smelled the milky stench of them, heard their cloying lullabies. For most, I have been nightmare, the beating wings and hellish screech that ruptures the soft skin of their mawkish contentment.

But for some, I am the black answer to their most secret prayers.

The first baby I strangled had little hands that wilted like tiny purple hyssop flowers as they fell limp to the ground. He was a boy, not yet circumcised. He was alone in the tent, wriggling in his bedding, his crow-haired mother gone to fetch water from the rain-flooded wadi. As my hands closed around his warm and flimsy neck, the mother was lifting her skirts, ankle-deep in coolness. She sighed with pleasure. Later, she would remember that. She would wail and rip the blue-black curls from her scalp, remembering how the sigh parted her lips, how the delight crawled her spine.

The pain of the mother was exquisite, even more delicious than that of the child.

But I soon discovered that some women breathed relief over the corpses of their young. They kept these breaths buried, sometimes hidden beneath tears, sometimes at the bottom of a great still numbness. It was a different flavor of hurt, the pain of a mother who fed too many mouths, or a mother who had been taken by force, a mother who was only a child. I collected these breaths and strung them as a necklace. They whispered, shifting and stirring at twilight, tugging at the thread that held them captive.

These breaths became my beloveds, my only companions.

Women learned from their grandmothers, they learned to dance the dark steps to keep me at bay. The ways were whispered in menstrual tents at the time of the hidden moon, shared over cooking fires, and at the water's edge as they bent to wash their clothes against the rocks. They hung amulets, they inscribed bowls. They buried the bowls at the entrances to their tents, later in the dirt beneath their doorposts. The same doorposts they would wash with blood to appease the Maker. They etched into their talismans and charms the names of the Messengers who had failed to win my obedience, the bright beings who cursed my womb and remade me as horror: *Senoi, Sansenoi, Semangelof*. Women pleaded for their guard. And yet, my name was scarcely written. It traveled in susurration over centuries, slipping from woman to woman, into ears and out of mouths, spoken in hush, passed along furtively, in fear. But it is written only once in the Maker's precious Book.

It is written that I will one day rest.

Kayin slew Hevel. He clutched a rock and split his brother's skull, left him to the fields, his blood howling in the earth and betraying his murder to the Maker. Kayin was cast out to wander, marked so all would know him and fear him. The Maker turned his eyes to blue. All of his children would bear that mark. He became a smith, a maker of metal things. He walked the earth and he walks it still. He took one of his sisters as his wife, and then another. The world teems now with his children. But I have always been his mate. I follow Kayin. I give him shelter in my body, under my wings, and then he journeys on. Through the wastes, through cities, through time. If I am to find rest, surely it will be when he does.

Until then, I hunger. And I hunt.

There are some grandmothers who remember me still. Old women who know my name, who hear it in the night as they ease their wretched bones into their beds. They hear it on the wind, they hear it in the stillnesses. They hear it in the insect song that named me, and in the lamentations of the owls. They hear my name, my desolation.

They tell their daughters, but rarely do daughters listen.

They tell that babies cry wild with distress because of my pinch at their toes, my sharp bites at their bulging bellies. Daughters smirk and the grandmothers hang their sterling heads. There are no more earthen bowls buried at thresholds. Few hang their charms and tie their red threads. Few mouth the names of *Senoi, Sansenoi, Semangelof.* They speak now of colic, of dairy intolerance, of Gastrointestinal Reflux.

They speak now of Sudden Infant Death Syndrome.

The grandmothers pray. They gnash their crumbling teeth. They hold up the gnarls of their knuckles to the Maker and beg for protection. For mercy. They mumble their tehillim and rasp out their tkhines. They spit against the Evil Eye, and they dare not call their granddaughters beautiful, dare not call their grandsons finely made. *Baruch Hashem* they say. *Baruch Hashem he's such an ugly baby.* They play at their tricks.

Ayin zahora they say. *Ayin zahora.*

But I watch and I wait. I smell the fresh flesh. I hear the pulse, the blooming and shrinking of small lungs. I arrive in so many disguises. I come cloaked in fevers. I twist in tiny bowels. I dry up milk, leave little mouths blistered. I spread rash and ruin. I inflame, I scar. I siphon away sleep. I lurk in cribs and cradles, steal breaths. I stifle and smother and strangle. I seduce mothers with madness.

Sometimes mothers wilt, and sometimes they burn.

I can be an undertow, seizing her ankles. Clinging with all the weight of the ocean. I can bury her in her own body. Drag her down into the depths of herself as she gasps and sinks like a stone. Her skin will be a prison. I can make the black substantial. I can make it fill the hollowed gorge of her belly, I can make it fill her eyes and mouth, clog her nose. I can rescind joy and annul hope. I can make her so very tired, so very heavy. Even the hair on her head will be a burden.

She will be saturated with sorrows.

But I can also be a bonfire, a rage, a ripping loose. I can make her run, jump, dance like a grinning puppet in flaming shoes. I can hurry her heart, and seed her dreams with terrors. Her veins will sting. I can fracture her vision and unhinge her every door, break her restraint, snap the tethers that keep her earthbound. Strip away her gravity. I can make her pinwheel without a name. Her very hands will be strangers to her.

She will be a wild waste, thrumming.

And the babies wail, the grandmothers beg. The noise moves me to rapture. All parts braiding to bring me the quickening, the culmination. The small corpse slack in my claws. The taste of death in my mouth. The knowledge that I have taken another child from Chava, another life that should have issued from mine. This is my only gladdening. I want only now to feel the next dissolution, the next life that will unspool beneath my wings. This is my satisfaction, the only allotted to me.

Surely, this the Maker has given me.

Mama loves the baby and the baby loves the mama

The ringing in Sarah's ears is ice, slamming against the back wall of her brain. One last push, and the rest of the baby slips out, the strange sensation of bonelessness following the hard fire of its emergent head. It slides onto the soaked sheets, cradled in the latex hands of the midwife. Sarah uncrimps her body, scrambles on all fours to snatch the wailing baby.

She sinks her teeth into its waxy leg. She tears the flesh, she gnaws the bone. Her hands are trembling, slick with viscera, her mouth full of its soft belly spilling, and she swallows. The midwife tries to wrench the baby's remains from her embrace, but Sarah growls, snaps. She hunches over the tiny corpse with animal eyes, heels to haunch.

Bones splinter between her teeth, and she swallows them too. All of it must be eaten. It's the only way. The only way to get the baby back into her belly, back into her body where it will be safe.

I'm leaving now Ben whispered, and Sarah jerked awake, her hands flying to feel for the baby. It was curled in her lap, eyes fluttering beneath closed lids, and Sarah exhaled, her fingers spreading loose, her molars unclenching. She'd had the dream again, the same nightmare she'd been having since the baby's birth.

Ben smiled at her now, gesturing toward the breakfast tray he'd brought. Scrambled eggs in a heaping pile, raisin toast thick with Irish butter. Orange juice. Bottled water. Ben was wearing his suit, his favorite tie, the one with turquoise swirls. After all these blurry days of seeing him only in his sweatpants and flannel shirts, he stood there looking like a stranger. Sarah tried not to cry, but it was useless. Crying was what she did now.

She'd been tough. But that had been in her twenties, when she was squatting in abandoned buildings, dumpster-diving for food and sleeping on a scrounged mattress. She'd gone soft as soon as she started eyeballing thirty, settling down into a real job, marrying Ben, gushing over IKEA highchairs. Her hard rind had split, she was all pulp. Since the birth, she was careening and slippery-eyed.

Her body was betraying her. She was hungry all the time. Her mouth filled with spit just looking at the raisin toast, but once again, the idea of eating anything recalled her nightmare, her mouth bloated with gore, and nausea made her stomach wavy.

What I could use is a cup of coffee she said, with a meek smile.

Ben tilted his head and gave her a look. That fucking infinitely patient look.

C'mon now, Rosie doesn't need any caffeine.

Sarah bit her lip. *Yeah* she said *but I do.*

No you don't, Mommy he said, massaging her shoulder.

Sarah was creeped out every time Ben called her *Mommy*, but she hadn't let on. It had started at the hospital, the loss of her name. All the nurses said *Mommy*.

How is Mommy feeling this morning? Has Mommy been charting the number of wet diapers? Did Mommy get any sleep?

Dry those eyes now Ben said, bucking her chin with his thumb.

He knew Sarah was frightened to be left alone with the baby for the first time. She'd said so a dozen times in the last few days, begging him to take more vacation time, but they'd reached the end of his allotment. His mother, Shirley, had flown in from New Jersey with the plan to stay two weeks to help with the baby, but after the first couple of days things had hit rock bottom with her. Shirley was fantastic at rocking the baby in the rocking chair and cooing, but little help otherwise. She'd hovered over Sarah as she'd nursed, wondering aloud when Sarah's milk would come in, sticking her pinky finger in the baby's mouth and sighing *Oh, she's so hungry! Look how she just keeps trying to suck!* Sarah told Shirley that sucking was just what babies do. But Shirley had kept on. Sarah blew her fuse as she was scarfing down her lunch on the third afternoon, when Shirley murmured sotto voce to the baby *Oh, you poor thing, I wish I had milk to give you, sweetie. I never had any trouble nursing my babies.* Sarah flung her plate across the room, shattering the china against the closet door, macaroni and cheese splattering onto the carpet.

Fuck you. Get the fuck out of my house she'd screamed, wrenching the baby from Shirley's arms.

Her husband had packed his mother back on a plane to Jersey the next morning, cooing apologies. As if Shirley was the one deserving them.

Ben nuzzled the baby carefully. He kissed Sarah goodbye with a dry pucker against her cheek and whispered *You'll be fine, you'll do great.*

He slipped out the front door into the morning dark. Sarah heard the deadbolt snap shut behind him as she sat in the bed, propped up by pillows, the breakfast tray still revolting. The television was humming low and throwing light on the walls. Her body was wreathed around the wriggling creature.

They'd all said *When you see the baby's face, you will fall in love.* They'd all said *You will fall in love like you've never known.* She'd been the last of her circle of friends to get pregnant for the first time, all those happily gravid and then puked-upon wives of Ben's co-workers and golf buddies, in their designer yoga pants, wielding snack tubes of pureed fruit with the ease and efficacy of ninjas distributing throwing stars. She'd envied them, she had. She'd wanted to push one of those six hundred dollar strollers and stick moist crayon-scribbled pages to the front of her refrigerator with alphabet magnets. She'd wanted a Sophie the Giraffe peeking out of the pocket of her overcoat, and the tote bag brimming with Eric Carle board books. She'd even wanted to bitch and moan while scrubbing the moldy innards of sippy cups with a toothbrush. She'd wanted to commiserate. It would be okay, they'd be in it together, in the sisterhood of motherhood. She'd wanted to be one of them. They'd had mountains of sage advice and comforting enthusiasms to heap upon her, cheering her along the home stretch as her belly swelled to the verge of bursting.

But it had been hardly golden so far. Sarah had come home from the hospital six days ago, barely sleeping since, and her limbs were heavy and numb. Six days since she'd gazed upon that fresh face with unparalleled expectation of joy, and yet the baby was still a stranger. A hungry stranger, with grasping hands and sucking mouth. She worried that she was fucking it all up. The baby's face was crisscrossed with wounds from its own sharp little claws. Sarah had been overzealous with the fingernail clippers, resulting in an I-heart-my-Mommy onesie so blood-spattered that she'd just hidden it in the bottom of the bathroom wastebasket and not even tried to get the stains out.

And now the front of Sarah's nightgown was stained with the milk that the baby called forth with the slightest mewl. She could smell the soured odor of it mingling with the musk of her damp armpits and the earthy stink that emanated from her crotch, from the blood that just didn't stop. She could still smell the scent of amniotic fluid on the baby's head, almost sweet, almost spicy. The mix of it all was overwhelming. *Grungy*. She'd had two showers in the last six days.

The baby would not tolerate being put down for an instant. Any time Sarah tried, it startled. Its arms flew rigidly into the ether and its eyes sprang open, its irises of darkest blue barely distinguishable from the hard black marbles of pupil. It slept only when clasped firmly in Sarah's arms, was quiet and appeased only when milk-drunk and unconscious. *It*. Sarah still could not manage to think *her*. Still could not wrap her mind around *Rosie*. She and Ben had decided to name the baby after Sarah's grandmother. They'd decided on that when the baby was just a minute riddle lodged deep in the briny murk of her pelvis.

The baby began rooting in its sleep. Its toothless mouth gaped open, working furiously, as it turned its head toward the solidity of Sarah's belly. She cupped a swollen and tingling breast as it gushed with milk, and guided the nipple to the baby's protruding tongue. She murmured over the tiny animal sounds of its feeding: *Rosie, Rosie, Rosie*. But the baby was still just an animal, a small woodland creature, soft grunting and smacking lips. She swiped clumsily with the back of her hand at the tears.

Sarah descended the stairs carefully, clutching the baby in both arms, its face pressed to her shoulder. She watched each slim step as she planted her foot firmly on it, peering over the crown of the baby's head. Her emptied belly sagged under the loose curtain of her nightgown. The house breathed from unseen lungs. She'd only been downstairs a few times since coming home from the hospital; she'd been denned down in the bedroom, Ben attending to her every need. He'd brought water, sandwiches, magazines. Now, she wanted that coffee. Strong and black and bitter.

Sarah padded into the kitchen, her bare feet chilled on the cold linoleum. She shifted the baby into a one-armed cradle and reached for the high cabinet above the stove to retrieve the coffee filters. The tips of her fingers only grazed the handle on the cabinet door. She rearranged the baby in the opposite arm, tried again to reach further, on the balls of her feet, to no avail. She huffed in frustration through her nose, and stared up at the cabinet helplessly, tears welling up again.

Sarah carefully set the baby on the countertop. Unencumbered, she managed to reach the filters, and then the canister of coffee grounds. The baby just lay there, completely helpless, unable even to roll over or lift its head. Sarah looked at it there, so utterly defenseless, lolling next to the knife block, and thought *Yes, it's exactly like a little animal. I could pick up that kitchen knife and open the belly with one quick slice.*

Sarah snatched up the baby, horrified. One hand cupped the diapered bottom and the other pinned its soft, breakable head to her shoulder. She began to pace the kitchen floor, twisting at the waist, firmly rocking the baby back and forth, murmuring over and over *Mama loves the baby and the baby loves the mama, Mama loves the baby and the baby loves the mama.*

Her heart rammed against her ribs.

Say it enough and it will be true she thought.

That was when she heard the scratching at the back door.

She walked in slow motion. She had time to notice the haze of the rising sun filtering through the inert kitchen curtains. There was a stillness, a color to the air. It made her think of Florida, of home and the eyes of hurricanes.

Scritch, scritch, scritch.

Holding the baby again in one arm, she slid the deadbolt open and pulled the door wide. Cold air billowed her nightgown, her naked legs trembling. It was a cat. A cat white as salt and odd-eyed. One eye blue and the other green. Sarah slammed the door with all her strength. The baby wailed, buckling against her body. Sarah stumbled backwards, knocking the canister of coffee from atop the stove to the floor. The lid popped off on impact, and the dark grit sprayed across the linoleum with a dry hush. Sarah fled, leaving the mess.

She scrambled, taking the stairs two at a time, the baby yowling in her grip. She shut the bedroom door behind her, locked it. She turned up the volume on the television to drown out the baby's noise. A deafening pizza commercial hammered her skull, TRIPLE CHEESE. The baby's screaming swelled. Sarah placed its worming body in the bassinet, and dug herself under the bedspread, covering her head with pillows. She hummed. Eventually, the baby cried itself to sleep. Sarah did, too.

When she opened an eye, her face half covered by the feather blanket, the bedroom was still suffused with morning light. It was quiet. Not just quiet, *silent*. The silence was absolute, thrumming. Her whole body was tight, and sore with silence. She'd felt it once before, dead quiet. When she had driven cross-country with some Food Not Bombs kids. She'd wandered off at a gas station in Wyoming, and it was so silent she'd felt like she was on the moon. She'd cracked. She'd never felt so alone. She'd never felt so *free*.

That was the silence now in her bedroom, the silence of the moon, of the absolute. Then she blinked, and heard the scratching. The sound of the cat, the white cat, in the walls. It was growing louder, digging closer. Her veins felt tight. She clamped her eyelids shut, and dug her fingernails into her palms. She started to evaporate. She could feel her molecules spreading, fleeing.

Then her whole body lurched violently, and a flood of noise hit the back of her neck and surged over her head, pushing her face under into the static.

The television. She'd left it on, turned up to top volume. Pizza commercial. *TRIPLE CHEESE*. Maybe she hadn't slept at all. Maybe she'd just rewound, looped back. The same commercial, the same moment in time, and…the baby. She couldn't look. She remembered the knife. The baby's hand folded softly as its arm lay on the kitchen counter. The knife had been in her hand, and there was blood streaked on the blade. But no, no, the knife had been in the wooden block.

She couldn't look at the baby. She averted her eyes and backed out of the bedroom, trailing her hand along the wall to the hallway. She wanted to look at her hand, see if it was wet with blood, if she was finger-painting the wall, but she couldn't turn her head. Her neck was knotted, her throat pinched shut. She stumbled into the bathroom and fell to her knees. The tub needed cleaning. Shirley hadn't done any housework. She'd held the baby and rocked in the rocking chair; she hadn't done the laundry or dug the hair from the drains. Sarah leaned over the rim of the tub and pushed her fingers into the hole, grasping for the snarl of scummy hair that collected there.

Her belly was tender, the porcelain hard against her, and she felt so emptied in there. The baby gone. She'd left the baby in the car at the gas station in Wyoming and that was stupid. Those kids didn't know what to do with a baby. The windows were up and it was hot. The lettuce was wilting in the fields. But no, that was California. The sweat on her neck. The windows were down, her hair had been whipping in the wind as she drove. The baby would be safe strapped in its car seat. But there had been no car seat, not yet. She and Ben had bought it at the Baby Depot, they'd disagreed on the color.

Sarah got out the bleach powder and the plastic scrubber, and began to scour the tub. She'd find the baby when the tub was clean. She'd go back, walk across the gravel at the gas pumps, across fire. The bathroom would be clean and she'd be a good mother, holding the baby in her arms like a sugar cube. She scrubbed until her knuckles were cracked and stinging, all the little hairs burned away. She stared at her hands, the skin pinked and taut. So clean. She retched into the toilet and bile scorched her throat.

It was so cold. Winter. Her nightgown. The paste of sweat on her skin. She pulled her legs up under the white fabric, grabbing her knees, and saw that there was a Rorschach-blot blood stain between her legs. She'd forgotten the pad, the lochia that wouldn't quit. She tried to rip the gown with her bare hands, tried to tear it off her body, but it wouldn't give. She pulled it over her head, struggling in the tangle, and buried it at the bottom of the wastebasket. Sarah buried her underwear too. She breathed, naked, standing.

She heard the baby crying. Sarah realized her breasts were hot rocks. She walked into the bedroom and turned off the TV. She looked into the bassinet and saw the baby. It was tight-fisted, a squall of desperate hunger. Milk dripped onto Sarah's bare belly.

She lifted the baby from its bedding and brought its open mouth to a nipple. It sucked fitfully at first, still caught in its sobbing, but settled into a solid rhythm of pull and swallow within minutes. It was quiet. Sarah stood before the front window, cradling the feeding baby and her heavy breast in her raw hands, as rivulets of blood basted her legs. Drops stained the carpet. There was a hushed patter as rain began to hit the glass. She watched the branches of the elm tree become jacketed with ice as the rain turned to sleet.

Sarah was holding the razor blade in her right hand, but she couldn't remember how it had gotten there. She stood in the hallway between the bathroom and bedroom and tried to walk it all backward. She tried to remember putting her clothes on, the leggings and oversize sweater and thick wool socks, but found herself snagging on something and falling. Hitting hard. She brought her hand to her nose, but she wasn't bleeding.

The baby was bound to her chest with the fitted sheet from her bed. It snored just audibly, living. Sarah didn't remember wrapping the baby in the sheet and tying it on to her body. She'd been standing at the window naked, nursing the baby to the hypnotic percussion of the icy rain, as she bled onto the carpet. The carpet. She'd wanted to clean the carpet before Ben got home.

It was already afternoon. She'd been afraid of him looming over the bloodstains, his eyebrows crinkled into an upper case V, reaching into his pocket for his phone to call Shirley and confess her ineptitude. He'd ask his mother to come back, he'd woo her onto a red-eye from Newark, and she'd be there the next morning, reeking of Shalimar and twittering at the baby with exaggerated sympathy.

There were scrub brushes and cleaning solutions in spray bottles scattered around the soiled carpet. She remembered then trying to read the label on the back of one of the bottles, and the letters swimming in her head, congealing to a hardened mass of nonsense. She'd given up and gone to the bathroom to find the razor blades in the medicine cabinet. She'd cut the dried blood from the pile of the carpet.

And so the razor in her hand, its straight sharp edge so close to the curving spine of the bundle cinched to her chest. Sarah could easily cut the baby with the razor, with any sharp object.

She saw beads of blood rising from pale skin, the slashes she'd made in her own arms in high school. She'd started wearing that ratty black sweater every day, long sleeves covering the evidence. The sweater was full of holes and runs pinched together with dozens of safety pins, and her mother threatened again and again to trash it. There was the day her mother grabbed Sarah by the wrist as she was stomping through the kitchen and tore the sweater over her head, revealing the stripes on her arms and her carved belly. Flakes of scab fluttered down to the linoleum while her mother wept and asked *Why?* but Sarah had had no answer. Nothing she could bear to confess to her sainted mother.

She scrambled now to gather the rest of the razor blades from the bathroom, along with all three pairs of scissors in the house. The staple remover, the seam ripper, the nail clippers, the pushpins from the bulletin board in Ben's home office. Sarah bundled them all in a dishtowel, securing the awkward lump of terrycloth with rubber bands, and buried it deep in the kitchen trashcan. She then got to work rearranging the furniture in the bedroom.

She shoved the bookcase away from the wall and turned the bed so that it obscured the mess under the window, but in the process she bled through her stretch pants and woke the baby. Sarah laid out a few clean towels on the mattress and sat to unbind the creature and give it suck. As the baby latched on, she thought of the bundle hidden in the trash, and for a split second panicked, thinking that she had somehow secreted the swaddled baby at the bottom of the can and was mistakenly holding the dishtowel of metal things clutched to her breast. She was breathing quickly and shallowly, but then she laughed at herself. Of course she would notice if she was nursing a towel full of scissors and thumbtacks. Of course she'd never shove the baby down beneath apple cores and crumpled paper towels and moldy curry chicken. Or at the very least, she'd notice what she was doing if she did. No. No, of course she'd never. She laughed again out loud, as Ben walked into the bedroom.

He beamed to see Sarah dressed and sitting on the bed cradling the baby to her breast.

Hey cuties he said. *Whatcha laughing about? How was your day?*

Sarah hadn't heard him coming through the front door. Usually she heard the deadbolt slide open, and the door slamming behind him. Usually she could hear it from anywhere in the house. But there he was, darkening the bedroom doorway, and before she could sputter out an answer to either of his questions, he was barreling ahead with more.

Do you realize you left a mess all over the kitchen floor? Hey, did you move the bed?

She opened her mouth to say something, anything, but her lips just flopped. The cat darted over the threshold and wound itself in a slow figure-eight around Ben's ankles.

What the fuck, Ben?! Sarah jumped from the mattress.

Yeah he laughed. *Surprise! We have a house guest. Poor guy was at the back door going nuts. It's so nasty out there, I figure—*

Absolutely not. Get it out.

You don't like cats? C'mon, it's sleeting out there if you haven't noticed.

Not that cat. No. Put it out. I don't want it here, I don't want it near the baby.

The cat won't harm the baby.

Sarah flared her nostrils as the cat rubbed its head against Ben's shins and flashed its mismatched eyes.

My grandmother used to say that a cat would steal a baby's breath if it got in the cradle she said, still firmly holding the baby to her body.

And why would she say that? Did your parents have a cat?

Yes, there was a cat that slept in my crib with me.

But nothing bad happened. Old wives' tale.

Maybe you should have more respect for old wives and their tales she snapped.

Ben stood silent for a moment and then scooped up the cat in his arms. He rubbed his thumb along the bony ridge on top of its head.

You're being silly. I'm not putting the cat out, not in this weather. The cat stays.

He turned his back on Sarah and walked out of the bedroom. She wanted to throw something after him and knock him in the skull, but she stood there with her hands full of baby, her legs coursing with electricity. She kicked the bassinet as hard as she could.

What are you going to feed the animal? she screamed after him. *Where do you think it'll shit?*

I'm going next door to borrow some food and litter from John until I go out tomorrow he yelled back upstairs.

And what do you think you're going to put the litter in? she called down.

I'll cut a cardboard box. Christ, Sarah, it's not such a big deal. Calm down, will you?

Sarah heard the front door slam behind him, and she dropped the baby onto the bed and raced downstairs to the kitchen. She dug through the trashcan frantically. Pulling the rubber bands off her hidden bundle, she unwrapped the dish towel. She placed a razor blade on the counter and rewrapped, reburied the cache. She tore back up the stairs, set the blade on the top of the baby's little bureau, and scooped the wailing infant into her arms. She stood well away from the razor, on the opposite side of the room, rocking the baby in her arms and shushing it until she heard the front door again.

Here, I found a razor blade for your boy she shouted.

She could hear Ben ascending the stairs. He was walking so slowly, as if it was deliberate. It seemed almost ominous. Was it really Ben, or an intruder? She began chewing on the inside of her lip. If Ben was trying to scare her, it wasn't funny at all.

Then there he was, just Ben, standing at the bedroom threshold, a Mason jar of kibble in one hand and a freezer bag of cat litter in the other.

You are acting weird he said.

I don't want that cat here, but I also don't want it shitting all over my house.

Still he said. *You're being weird.*

He stood there, not saying anything more, just looking at the wrecked bassinet. The fitted sheet was still pulled off the bed and lay in a heap beside it. The ice against the window pane got louder. His eyes were mottled with suspicion. He shifted his weight from one leg to the other, and Sarah could hear the floor groan underneath him.

Why did you move the bed? he asked.

The baby ruffled its arms, it was a little bird in Sarah's grip. The sound of feathers. The elm branches scraped against the siding behind her.

We could shatter the glass she thought. *We could break the window and the baby would fly away.* The baby would be a red-bellied robin in the snow and Sarah would scatter bread crumbs. Soak the bread crumbs in her milk and toss them into the cold wind.

Sarah?

She remembered the first time they met, Ben testing the heft of a melon in the health food store where she'd worked. She'd told him to smell the stem scar, smell the sweet perfume of its ripeness. He'd done it and smiled, offered a handshake and introduction. She'd wiped her hands on her denim apron and taken his hand in hers. He was the kind of guy who shook hands. The kind who made confident eye contact, and wore ties. The kind of guy who had more pairs of shoes than she did, and had never eaten out of a dumpster. And yet. When she rang up his purchases and he asked her for her phone number, Sarah had written it down on the back of his receipt.

Sarah?

He was standing in the doorway of their bedroom. He wasn't a stranger.

Look, babe, you must be exhausted. Let me take Rosie and you can have a nice hot shower and lie down for a while.

For their first date, they'd gone out for sushi and a movie. Sarah had been twenty-nine, and it was the first proper date she'd ever been on. He'd brought flowers to her door, and kissed her goodnight at the end. Within a year, she was standing at the altar wearing a dress that cost more than any car she'd ever owned. A year after that, a midwife wearing a Venus of Willendorf pendant was plopping the vernix-crusted baby onto her chest. Ben had wept with joy at the wedding and at the birth. He was a great husband. He was a great father. If Sarah didn't love him, she was crazy.

The cat slinked through the bedroom doorway between Ben's legs and then started circling him, meowing insistently, eager for the kibble in the jar.

No Sarah said. *You take care of your cat. I'll take care of my baby.*

The walls breathed. Sarah hovered in the center of the hallway, shying from either side, as the plaster pulsed, slick and alive. She'd slipped out of the bedroom once Ben was snoring, left the baby sleeping safely on its back, body slack and sheathed in pink fleece. She wasn't tired. She hadn't felt tired since she'd hidden under the covers that afternoon and cried herself to sleep. *Invincible.* She wasn't hungry either. She'd told Ben to go ahead and have a plate of leftovers for dinner. She'd lied and said that she had just fixed herself a big sandwich before he'd come home. It would be just one more thing that wouldn't seem right to him. Another reason to call his mother, another reason to appraise Sarah. His eyes were menacing her. He knew she was a bad mother. *Wicked.*

She'd been lying in bed, just waiting for the baby fall asleep in the crook of her arm. Waiting for its sucking mouth to slow and stop, so she could flee. She'd heard the breathing in the walls, felt the respiration of the house, its turning into something other, something warm and waking.

Now the floor rumbled beneath Sarah's feet, the hall carpet buckling. Shadows twitched. They were sinewy, unrippable. Doorframes were arching ribs. Whale bones. The house groaned and heaved. She grasped the bannister with both hands, staring down the whale's throat. There was nothing in her belly, no heavy thing to ballast her, no more baby, and she felt herself weightlessly sliding. Sliding whole into the black gut of the giant. At the foot of the stairs she raised her eyes, surprised to see that all of her living room furniture had been swallowed too.

All of her things, or maybe just replicas of them, floated in the watery darkness. Glints quivered through the ripples; the shine of a mirror, the spiny edge of a bookend, the teeth of a zipper on a jacket hung at the door. Sarah treaded through the sunken quiet. Everything shifted in waves and the walls contracted. The floor was littered with pale naked knucklebones and undigested teeth. She tried not to disturb them, but they rattled as she walked. They trembled from within, like jumping beans. A roar started from above as their shaking grew frenzied, and a great sluice of shadow rushed down the stairwell, flooding the living room and lifting Sarah to kiss the ceiling.

Choking, she panicked, her heartbeat clattering. She swam for the kitchen. She thrashed. She thought only of breathing again, of stopping the pain in her chest. She raged, but her ankles were snagged by the undertow. She became heavy pieces of herself. She went down. She stopped fighting the weight, and opened her eyes in eerie calm. Her heart made no song. Her lungs were saturated and still. She spread into the silence.

Her houseplants swayed as if asleep, in blue underwater light. Ben's dirty dinner plate rose from the table, tilting. The dining room chairs somersaulted by in slow-motion. She watched them turn and disappear. Then all around her there was sparkling phosphorescence. A million tiny lights floating, like swallowed stars riding the currents, ascending and descending. They wriggled up and dove down. They whipped and danced. She reached out her fingers to touch them and they squirmed away from her. Then they closed in around her and tickled against her skin.

Sarah spun and she was standing on the kitchen linoleum, cold with sweat. The cat was crouched by the stove, its back a drawn bow. It was spectral in the dark. Sarah's toes were numb and she was suddenly again aware that she was bleeding from her womb. That she was emptied, wounded. Her arms hung at her sides. The cat hissed.

This is my house she said. *Mine.*

She licked her front teeth beneath the cover of her lip.

The tip of the cat's tail flicked.

Sarah lunged toward the animal and it skittered backwards. She chased it toward the cellar door, its claws scrabbling. She opened her mouth and the sound that emerged was not human. *Dominance.* She grabbed the broom from behind the trash can and wielded it white-knuckled. The cat bristled and swiped. Sarah reached for the knob on the door and it took its chance, raking her ankle as it bolted between her legs and shot back across the linoleum toward the dining room. She howled and clutched at the scratch, dropping the broom and sliding one-footed in her wool sock. The back of Sarah's skull smacked the kitchen floor.

She lay still, her eyes tracing the cracks in the sagging popcorn finish of the ceiling.

You don't belong here she said quietly to the cat.

The white cat with odd eyes.

It is a white streak moving through the park at dusk, a comet plunging into the dense congregation of trees. The boys are chasing after it. The boys' concert t-shirts make their backs smudges of black on black, camouflaged in the dark of the pines. Their legs in black jeans turn almost invisible. They are vanishing. Sarah is running, a few strides behind. She is now always a few strides behind her boys. Sarah's body is swelling, changing shape and making her other. She's bleeding for the first time, the bulk of the adhesive pad shifting and rubbing between her thighs as she runs. She doesn't want the boys to know it. They became blood brothers without her. They said *Don't be dumb. You can't be anybody's brother.*

The damp earth beneath the grass squishes with each of Sarah's footfalls. Her knee meets the ground, and wet cold soaks through her jeans. One of the boys passes the knife. The handle fits perfectly in her fist. She is not just some girl. She can and will match their cruelty without flinching. She presses the point against the cat's body, through its skin, between its ribs, through its muscle and organs. It is easy and smooth. No need to push hard. The cat doesn't claw or bite. It doesn't make a noise at all, besides its purring. It purrs louder and louder, like a swarm of bees.

Sarah knelt on the kitchen floor, her hands poised in the air, arrested mid-stab. The back of her head throbbed. She coughed and the pain radiated. A firework. In her brain. She needed something to clean. She pulled the scrub brush from under the kitchen sink and pushed its hard plastic bristles rhythmically against the curves of the chrome basins. The motion was soothing, the action of scrubbing.

She had scrubbed at the stain on the knee of her jeans, the mud and green of kneeling to kill the cat. She'd poured blue liquid detergent on the blotch, in her mother's laundry room.

She'd scrubbed until her arms and knuckles hurt. It never came completely clean. Sarah had made the jeans into shorts. But even then, the stain was like a phantom limb.

Come to bed.

Ben's voice startled her. She dropped the brush, it clattered in the sink as she spun.

The icicles on the gutters had been melting all morning, the steady loud slapping of dripping water sounding like a man masturbating. Once she'd thought it, she couldn't unthink it. It turned her stomach. She'd bundled up the baby and herself. She stood on the front porch with the door locked behind her. Sarah was afraid to drive the car. Afraid of roads that might still be icy, afraid of having to properly install the infant car seat. She knew that she was going on foot.

There was a coffee shop off the main drag, maybe a fifteen minute walk, down past the gas station. That meant east and then south. She'd be walking into the sun, and maybe that would make the trek warmer. Imagining the smell of coffee propelled her. She would sit anonymously in the cozy café with a hot latte between her palms. She'd lay the baby down on the cushioned window seat, among the mismatched brocade throw pillows. Nobody would know her name.

But maybe somebody would ask. They'd ask for the baby's name too, and she would force herself to say it. Her lips would make all the right motions. *Rosie.*

Sarah negotiated the front steps carefully, the chunks of de-icing salt crunching beneath her boots. The baby was silent. She wondered if its eyes were open, but she couldn't tell. Looking down she could only see the pink wool hat. Sarah held the lump in the front of her coat with two yellow-mittened hands and headed down the front walk. The chill of the air felt good in her lungs. She inhaled deeply. It was easier to think outside of the house.

It hadn't snowed for a couple of weeks but there were still dirty mounds of iced-over snow at the intersections of the residential roads. Blackened crags rising against the curbs, around which she needed to maneuver. Cracked white puddles, thawed beneath the surface, that shouldn't be walked on. Sarah watched her feet, started counting her steps, and then couldn't stop. Fifty-five, fifty-six, fifty-seven…

Her boots made a soft scuffing rhythm against the concrete. She was starting to sweat beneath her fleece and mittens. She wanted to start stripping off layers, but then she'd have the baby loose in her arms and all the useless garments as well. She imagined leaving a trail of clothes behind her as she walked, abandoning her jacket on somebody's front lawn, her sweater snagged in a hedge of prickly holly that separated a corner lot from a cross-street, her boots left slumping empty in the gutter. She imagined the baby, set safely in the low crotch of a leafless crepe myrtle as she walked into the glare of the sun, nude. It would be silent.

The baby stirred under her jacket and started smacking its lips as it rooted for her breast. She walked faster. She exaggerated the bounce in her step and hoped the motion would lull the baby back to sleep. Eighty-seven, eighty-eight, eighty-nine…

The minivan stopped in the road ahead of Sarah and the baby. The passenger window slid down with electric smoothness, and for a second she didn't recognize the face of the woman shouting her name in surprise.

Sarah! Hey, Sarah! I thought that was you! Where are you going?

It was Sarah's instinct to bolt. Her eyes flashed down the cross-street, hoping for an escape route, but it was a cul-de-sac.

Hey Nina. I was just taking a walk. With the baby.

They make strollers for that, you know Nina laughed. *And it's cold! Do you want a ride home? I just have to drop off the littles at school first.*

No, no I'm okay to walk. I needed some fresh air. I had to get out of the house.

Nina was the wife of Ben's co-worker Nate. She wore big funky earrings and was always lipsticked in red. Sarah liked that about her. She had two kids in elementary school, Hazel and James, and an older son from a previous marriage, Ernesto, who was maybe in the eighth grade now. He had been getting mustachey the last time Sarah had seen him. Nina was smiling at Sarah now, and she could hear the click of the passenger side door unlocking.

Seriously, Sarah. I want to see that new baby. Get in, already.

There's not even a car seat.

Nina sighed. *We're going less than a mile. Get in the back between the boosters. I'll go super slow.*

Sarah stood rooted to the pavement, unsure. She was bouncing in place she realized, patting the baby's back with one yellow mitten. It seemed like such a motherly gesture. She'd seen other mothers do it countless times. So strange that she'd do it too, without thinking. Nina tapped the horn and Sarah jumped.

Look Sarah, I know we don't really know each other very well, but you might need a little grown-up company? I know what it's like with a newborn. It's tough. Get the hell in the minivan.

Sarah couldn't see Hazel and James in the backseat through the window tint, but she heard them tittering.

Yeah, Mommy said hell. It's a grown-up word and I'm a grown-up.

I just wanted to get a coffee Sarah mumbled, but she climbed into the mini-van, squeezing between the two giggling grade-schoolers. She felt a strange sense of relief. Nina twisted in her seat and pawed gently at the baby-lump in Sarah's fleece. Her eyes shined expectantly. As Sarah unzipped her jacket, Nina trilled.

Oh my freaking God, Sarah. She is so precious. My ovaries ache. I want to eat her up.

Sarah winced. Her dream.

Nina wriggled a finger under the baby's chin and pinched softly. *Yes, I could eat you up!*

Sarah slapped her hand away. Her heart was speeding. The sweat from her walk was cold on her neck.

Nina looked at Sarah, tilting her head to the side just slightly. Her big cloisonné teardrop earrings shifted and dangled. Her red lips parted slowly. Sarah fought the urge to grab the door handle, run.

Are you feeling okay, Sarah?

Nina's voice was starlight breaking. Raining down tinkling. Sarah felt it like crushed glass underneath her as she squirmed between the booster seats. Nina's eyes wouldn't leave Sarah's face, and Sarah didn't know where to look.

No hitting said Hazel emphatically. *Use your words.*

I'm feeling just fine.

Are you sure, Sarah? Is anybody helping you at home?

You should say 'sorry' said James.

I'm fine. The baby's fine.

I'm going to bring you a casserole.

That's really not necessary.

I'd like to help you.

I'm fine.

There was an increasing pressure behind Sarah's eyeballs. They might pop out of her skull and onto her lap. They would roll under the front seat and disappear among desiccated Cheerios. James wiped his nose on the sleeve of his coat, leaving a long snail trail on the Gore-Tex.

I think I'm just going to walk home Sarah said.

Nina shook her head and her earrings bounced against her jaw.

No, let me drop you off.

Nina spun back around to the steering wheel and put the minivan in gear before Sarah could muster protest.

You are kidnapping me Sarah sighed.

Nina drove slowly as promised, inching along toward the kids' school. Sarah clutched the baby tight, and kept her gaze locked on the road in front of them. As they approached the elementary school, traffic clogged the street. At least a hundred minivans and station wagons jockeyed for position in the drop-off lane. Sarah took a deep breath and shut her eyes for a minute. She didn't want to be left alone in the vehicle with Nina. She didn't want to continue their conversation. She'd wanted that hot cup of coffee. She'd wanted to escape the house, but now she wanted to scurry back and hide there. She wanted to lay the baby in its bassinet and curl herself into a tight ball under her comforter. They were not safe here. *Not safe!*

Sarah's eyes flew open just in time to see the cat. The white cat, darting in front of the minivan.

Watch out! she screamed, grabbing at Nina's shoulder.

Nina slammed on the brakes, screeching to a full stop, her earrings swinging. Half a second later, they were hit from behind.

I didn't see any cat, Sarah.

Well, I did. I saw it run right in front of us, then it disappeared under that parked car.

Okay, well, will you just get back in the van?

Abso-fucking-lutely not.

Sarah stood at the curb, the top of her breast exposed to the cold, as her fleece flapped open and she cradled the nursing baby in her arms.

You could just sit in the van until Rosie finishes her feed. I won't drive.

Fuck no.

It had been a minor collision, yes. A little bump in the rear. Nina and the momentarily irate dad with the Bluetooth earpiece and the Orioles ball cap hadn't even exchanged insurance information. The guy had paced back and forth a few times in his pajama pants, looking from one bumper to another, then shrugged his shoulders and waved Nina off impatiently as he continued his phone conversation.

Yeah, yeah, I told you it's got to be Fed-Exed today. This morning.

Sarah had sat paralyzed in the minivan, scared to emerge and let anybody see that the baby hadn't been safely strapped into a car seat. She had slouched between James and Hazel, scrunching her eyes tightly closed and wishing the earth would open to swallow her. The baby was just fine. It wasn't even crying, until Bluetooth Guy had gone on his way to the drop-off lane and Sarah had sprung from the van and started walking briskly in the other direction. Nina had caught up to her a few blocks away, after letting the kids out. By that time, the baby was crying, and Sarah had surrendered to unbuttoning her blouse right there in the street.

Nina leaned her forehead on the steering wheel, between her ten-and-two hands. She groaned.

Sarah, I can't just leave you here on the side of the road. I'm going to call Ben.

Are you crazy? Do NOT tell Ben about any of this. He will freak out.

And what am I supposed to do?

Just go home.

I don't think you're okay.

Sarah looked up at the sky. She popped the baby off her breast and zipped them both back up inside her jacket. She was sure she'd seen the cat dart in front of them. She was one hundred percent certain.

What are you going to do? Follow me home?

I guess that's my best option.

Sarah walked as quickly as she could along the sidewalk and Nina trailed almost alongside, idling down the quiet streets. She kept the passenger-side window rolled down and Sarah could hear the burble of talk-radio voices. The baby snored softly against her chest. She felt a wet spot of drool spreading. *Rosie.* Sarah tried saying it to herself as she walked, *Rosie Rosie Rosie*, in rhythm with her boots. It had rolled so easily off of Nina's red lips. Nina was a great mom.

Rosie, my daughter. Rosie, her name. She, she, she. Rosie.

By the time Sarah was standing in front of her house, reaching out a hand to lean against the elm tree, the name was a word she had repeated until it lost all meaning. Until it sounded foreign. She saw it written a thousand times in transparency, overlaying everything everywhere she looked, but its letters spelled nothing at all.

Nina pulled into the driveway and got out of the van as Sarah shut her eyes and tried to piece the name together. R connected to the O connected to the S… The blackness was vertiginous. Sarah retched into the English ivy.

Nina's hands were on her shoulders, she was walking up the front steps, one foot in front of the other. Nina reached into Sarah's jacket pocket and found the house keys. Sarah could hear the jangle of them though her eyes were unfocused.

Hey, it's okay. Let's get you inside. Let's get the baby set down safe.

Sarah was looking up at Nina. Her earrings were like wind chimes without sound. Nina was unzipping her fleece, lifting the baby carefully from her chest. The warmth of its body gone. She could see the baby in Nina's arms but she couldn't hear it. Again, the silence.

Nina had opened more than Sarah's jacket. She had cracked open her ribs, split her like a fruit or a crustacean. She'd lifted the baby from inside Tabitha, raised the baby into the light, and now Sarah was receding. Sliding between the strata of blacks and grays, reaching out her arms. She fought to unfasten her lips. *Rosie.* It was a creak. *Rosie.* She was caught between the colors. A membrane closed around her. Sarah was absorbed.

She heard their voices with her eyes closed. Nina's words and Ben's too, skidding and hushed.

Mother of God, Ben. How long has it been since she's slept? Or eaten?

I...I don't know for sure. They said 'Sleep when the baby sleeps' and the baby's always sleeping...

Is she eating?

Look, I don't know. I don't know.

I think she's probably dehydrated, too. Her lips. Look at how dry her lips are.

Sarah could feel them both dropping their gazes to the couch. She breathed evenly, kept her eyes shut, her brow relaxed.

Wasn't her mother supposed to come help?

No, no, it was my mother. Her mother is...she doesn't talk to her parents much. My mother was here, but they...Sarah kicked her out.

So she's just been alone in the house all day?

Nina, I don't know what you expect me to say here. I can't quit my job, okay? I thought she was doing just fine. She got weird about the cat, but—

The cat? You mean the cat that was shut in the closet upstairs? Yeah, I met that cat. I cleaned up after it, once I put Rosie down.

Had Sarah trapped the cat? She couldn't remember. She tried to sit but her head was still swimmy. Her throat was thick with mucus. The words were a gurgle.

Her. Rosie.

Nina and Ben's conversation stopped abruptly. They both rushed to Sarah.

Ben lifted a tumbler of ice water from the coffee table. He held it in his hand awkwardly, obviously wanting to thrust it at her, as he said *Hey, sweetie. Hey, how are you feeling?*

Rosie Sarah repeated. *Rosie.*

She's upstairs said Nina. *She's sleeping. She's good.*

She's good Sarah echoed.

You want a drink of water, sweetheart? The glass was sweating in Ben's hand. Sarah pulled herself up to sitting and kneaded the top of her right breast, pushing on a hard tender spot that was almost in her armpit. She winced.

I've got to feed her.

You drink that water and I'll get the baby up Nina said. *Why don't you just sit with her Ben?*

Should I make you a sandwich? Ben asked. *Or maybe some scrambled eggs?*

Sarah shook her head. She heard Rosie whimpering, and the sound of Nina's footsteps on the stairs. They descended, perfect to look at. Nina could be this baby's mother. A flurry of tiny fingers reached for Nina's bright curving lips. It was rooting for Nina's breast. A breast was a breast. Sarah was only a body, only food. She could walk away. Sarah could run for her life, and the baby would thrive without her. Her heart was beating in her throat, in her used belly.

Nina was almost to the bottom of the stairs when the cat flashed down, streaking underfoot. As Nina fell, baby in one arm, grabbing for the bannister with the other, the cat raced through the living room and dining room toward the kitchen. Nina hit the step hard with her tailbone. The baby let out a sharp cry. Ben rushed to the stairs, but Sarah sprang to her feet and bolted after the animal. She felt herself surge. *Mama loves the baby.*

The kitchen linoleum is a swamp of twisted bedsheets, damp with the blood and sweat of birth. It bogs around Sarah's ankles. Her body has produced this odd-eyed thing instead of a baby. This white monster, all hiss and fury. She seizes it by the scruff of its neck and it thrashes, baring its claws and twisting to bite. She opens the back door and the cold air slaps her face. It's the only way, to thrust it out. She flings the cat as far as she can, as hard as she can. It hits the dirt in a scrambling mass of fang and fur. It is a chalk mark in the gathering dark. She clutches the back door with a shaking hand. As she slams it shut, for a splinter of a second, she sees herself, naked and pale, crouched in the cat's place. This is the work, the war work. There is no ceasing. She will keep hurling the animal out, crushing the animal down, for as long as it takes to keep her—*her, Rosie*—safe.

Sarah pressed her body to the door and spoke through it. *You, you don't belong here.*

Sheitel

When Yitzy gets home from work on Friday afternoons, the floors are swept, the challah is baked, and the children are bathed. Their hair smells like shampoo, and it's combed back from their faces neatly, wetly. They clamor at the baby-gate at the top of the stairs when he comes through the front door. They squeal with delight *Abba Abba Abba* as he pauses to touch the mezuzah and bring his fingertips to his lips.

There's a roasted chicken in the oven, eight pieces with crisp skin, arranged on a bed of sliced mushrooms and bay leaves swimming in olive oil. He wheels his bicycle down to the basement, and as he passes through the kitchen, he gives her a quick kiss, his lips pleasantly dry and warm, or tugs on her apron strings playfully. His beard smells of sawdust.

For this Shabbos, there are fresh green beans simmering on the stovetop. Last Shabbos it was carrots, cut into thick orange coins. The week before, broccoli. The week before that, it was Brussels sprouts thinly sliced, sautéed in a pan. Before that, green beans.

Our sages say that Shabbos exists outside of time, that each day of rest and prayer and peace is but a taste of the World to Come. The Olam haBa is an infinite progression of Shabboses strung together, days perfectly stitched, whole and holy, into one splendid garment. From darkness to darkness like womb to tomb, but stretching much further in both directions, until they wrap around.

If you look far enough, with a telescope strong enough, you'll realize you are viewing the back of your own head.

When everything else is ready, she climbs the stairs slowly, with deliberation, and takes her bath. She likes the water very hot. She dresses, in a black dress, or a blue one. She waits until the very last minute to do the very last thing. It's there, brown waves tumbling around the featureless Styrofoam face, waiting for her. She tucks all her hair into the wig cap and takes it in her hands. Her sheitel.

She's begun to wear it less and less. Now she puts it on only for Shabbos. During the week, she reaches for a tichel instead. She tells Yitzy she's decided to keep it special for Shabbos, and it will last longer that way. *We don't have the money to replace it.* She tells her girlfriends it's just easier to tie a headscarf and be done with it. *And have you seen these gorgeous new tichels Miriam is selling?*

What she doesn't tell is that when she wears the sheitel, she hears things.

She's come to pick up her older daughter from Hebrew lessons when Rabbi Mendlowitz calls to her from his study. His door is open, his books line the walls, deep brown leather with gold embossed alef-beis gleaming on every spine. He beckons with two fingers held aloft, gestures for her to sit.

She's keenly aware that the blouse she's wearing today doesn't quite cover her collar bones. She sits with her arms crossed awkwardly, because she sees, glancing down, that the tattoo on her forearm is peeking from her up-rolled sleeve. It's the letter shin, pinkly inked to nearly match her skin tone, so that it appears to be almost a birthmark. She's never sure whether to be less or more embarrassed by the fact that it's a Jewish tattoo. Either way, it's an indelible remnant of her former life, and a constant cause for suspicion. She is a ba'al teshuvah, after all, not born into the observant life, and she could backslide, God forbid, at any moment.

Rabbi Mendlowitz's black eyes sparkle, and his cheeks are always flushed.

So he says *my son tells me your Esther has said something strange to him.*

She swallows, and nods. He goes on.

She tells him that God speaks to her. She says that you told her that she can listen and that Hashem will talk to her.

She clears her throat. Well, in a way, yes. Don't you think?

He smiles broadly. *No.* He shakes his head vigorously, and his payos tremble, the little spiral curls flopping against his reddened earlobes. *No, Hashem spoke to prophets, and there are no more prophets. Are you thinking that Hashem has something personal to say to you? This is not so much a Jewish idea.*

She tugs at her sleeve. No, no of course not, it's just that I meant for her to know that we should all be listening to that "still small voice"...you know, inside, to figure out what God wants of us...

Rabbi Mendlowitz smiles again, wide enough so that his face is split, honey pouring golden from the rock. *Torah! Torah tells us exactly what Hashem wants of us! Voices are for the prophets! Torah! We have Torah to tell us how to live!*

Yes she says. *Yes, of course, Rabbi.*

He ushers her out of his study with a hand that hovers six inches from her shoulder. She gathers Esther from her classroom and they walk the three blocks home. She thinks the whole way about what she didn't tell him.

Our sages say that when Ya'akov saw the angels, the messengers, ascending and descending the ladder on the banks of the Yabbok, they were *ascending* first because they are always here, always among us. The man he wrestled with, the man who wrenched his hipbone from its socket, the man he wrestled with when he was alone, was already there.

Rachel Rosenberg is her best friend, and they are in the supermarket, inspecting packages of plastic-wrapped kosher turkey legs when she finally broaches the subject. She tells her just that she keeps getting a song stuck in her head, a song she used to know, that it might be stress. She doesn't implicate the sheitel.

Rachel raises one diligently groomed eyebrow and her lips swerve with a wicked crook.

Is it...sexy?

No, no she says. *It's just a Bob Dylan song. He's a poet, practically. He's Jewish, you know.*

Well, I don't know from Bob Dylan says Rachel *but what's it called?*

She replaces a one-pound tube of hamburger meat on the refrigerated shelf and sighs *All Along the Watchtower*.

Rachel Rosenberg's skirt swishes, the hem dragging on the battered linoleum as they walk down the aisle lined with glass jars in which colorless blobs of gefilte fish brood silently.

Look says Rachel *I'm sure it is just stress. You have such a meshugganah life. Why do you want to stay home with the baby, anyway? It's way past time for you to get another job. You need to feel useful. You need to do something with yourself. Why don't you teach again? You're great with the kinderlach.*

She laughs through her nose. She doesn't explain. Rachel Rosenberg doesn't know from ironic.

The tops of Dr. Bloch's breasts are visible today, draped in yellow silk patterned with tiny blue birds. When she smiles, both of her glossy lips curl perfectly into the shape of a little red boat. She keeps getting distracted by the little red boat.

I can't write you a prescription for the Xanax again until you are finished nursing Dr. Bloch says *but if you feel like you are experiencing depression, there are options. There are definitely anti-depressants that are considered safe to take while breastfeeding.*

She shifts uncomfortably on the exam table, and the paper crinkles loudly beneath her. *No, no, it's not depression. It's just anxiety again, I think. I mean, I'm not having panic attacks, not like before I had my gall bladder out. I'm just, well, I have headaches, not really pain, but just pressure, just sometimes. And I feel like I, I don't know, I worry.*

She doesn't want to try to fit her sheitel into Dr. Bloch's little red boat. She wonders how many angels could squeeze in there, anyway. It would capsize.

What you could try Dr. Bloch says *is taking Benadryl. It's an antihistamine, and that will relieve the stress response just as it relieves an allergic reaction. It's just fine for breastfeeding, and it will help you sleep, too.*

But won't an antihistamine reduce my milk supply? she asks. She thinks she's read that somewhere. It dries up fluids.

It may affect it slightly, or it may not. But you have to weigh the risks and the benefits.

Dr. Bloch's little red boat bucks as if on high seas. She uncrosses and recrosses her legs. The skirt is short, the legs are sleek and sheathed in flesh-toned nylon. She wears a thin gold chain as an ankle-bracelet. It shows through the nylon.

The most important thing is that you are well, that you are a happy and healthy mommy. Isn't that right?

Yes, yes, of course, Doctor.

She drives home in the station wagon, and for the first time in a long, long while, she turns on the radio. It's all static, and she jabs at buttons blindly, hoping for a rock and roll station. As she hits the brakes for a stop sign, the song blares out of the back speakers, heavily skewed to treble. All Along the Watchtower. She leans her head against the steering wheel and cries, laughing.

She gets ready for the mikvah just as carefully as always, even though she hasn't bled in three cycles. Yitzy doesn't know. She switches back and forth between her bed and his right on schedule.

She washes her hair and trims her nails. She scrubs the soles of her feet and shaves her underarms. She soaks in her very hot bath, with no oils or salts. She uses plain soap. She doesn't put on deodorant after, or lotion. She brushes her teeth thoroughly, flosses between. She's as naked as the day she was born, but for the tattoo, the letter shin.

She walks the three blocks to the mikvah in the dark, her hands burrowed deep in her coat pockets. Orion is above her, that's the only constellation she can identify. She's taken two little hot pink Benadryl, and she feels slightly loose in the legs. She walks just a quarter inch above the pavement, her shoes make no sound.

The rebbetzin is waiting for her, a long gray snood bagging her ponytail. These nights, once a month, are the only times she's seen the rabbi's wife without her lovely blond sheitel.

She rinses her body in the shower stall, submits it to the rebbetzin's inspection. The rebbetzin pronounces her ready, free of any dirt or debris or random stray hair that might lodge between God and herself. But the rebbetzin's blue eyes dangle for a moment too long above her belly, swinging like divining pendulums, and they narrow.

Nu? So is it a boy or a girl?

Oh, oh no, I've just put on a little weight she stammers. She didn't think it was obvious yet, the swelling secret underneath the silvery striations of her old stretch marks.

The rebbetzin clucks. *Uhm-hmmm. Estie and Tzipi will be very happy to have a sister or a brother.*

She nods weakly, her subterfuge so easily defeated.

You haven't told Yitzy yet?

She shakes her head. *No.*

The rebbetzin nods. *And why not?*

It's just…well, it's my sheitel…

The rebbetzin stands, looking at her expectantly, but she can't finish the sentence.

She walks gingerly down the tiled steps into the mikvah, the warm water swallowing her ankles, her knees, her thighs. Her feet reach the bottom of the pool, she's shoulder deep. Her unbound hair floats on the surface, spreading out in a nimbus of deep brown eels. She recites the bracha and immerses once, twice, three times.

*Kosher…kosher…kosher…*the rebbetzin pronounces the word after each dunk, judging each satisfactory. And then she's left alone in the little room, left alone to reflect, to say her personal prayers.

She bends her knees, dropping down just so, so that the surface is just below her nose, the water covering her mouth. And she looks. She looks for any tiniest grain of sand, any fragment of dead skin, any lost hair that some other woman may have missed. Any other piece of any other woman's life that might be suspended in the warm womb of the pool. She listens for any secret the tiles might have absorbed. She listens for stowaway wishes

When Yitzy gets home from work on Friday afternoons, the floors are swept, the challah is baked, and the children are bathed.

Our sages say that two angels accompany a Jew on his way back home from shul on Friday nights. Two messengers, one good. And one of the yetzer hara, the dark side, the evil inclination, the animal soul. Two angels follow him home, and if the house has been properly prepared for making Shabbos, *the lamp lit, the table set, the couch spread*, then the good angel speaks a blessing that next Shabbos will be just the same, and the bad angel is compelled to answer *Amen*. If the house is not prepared, it is the evil angel that utters the wish, that next Shabbos should be the same, and the good angel then must agree, seal the curse with its own *Amen*.

There's a roasted chicken in the oven, eight pieces with crisp skin, arranged on a bed of sliced mushrooms and bay leaves swimming in olive oil. He wheels his bicycle down to the basement, and as he passes through the kitchen, he gives her a quick kiss, his lips pleasantly dry and warm, or tugs on her apron strings playfully. His beard smells of sawdust.

For this Shabbos, there are fresh green beans simmering on the stovetop.

When Yitzy gets home from shul, everything is ready. The candles are lit. She's wearing her blue dress, and her sheitel, carefully brushed.

They sing together, as always:

Shalom Aleichem, malachei ha-shareis malachei el yon
Mi-melech malachei ha-melachim Ha-Kadosh Baruch hu...
Peace be upon you, ministering angels, messengers of the most High
The King who reigns over kings, The Holy One, Blessed be He...

And she hears two songs. The lyrics mingle. They grapple. It's hard to tell what is what, who is who. She feels the baby move, low and deep in the crucible of her belly. Her hip hurts.

Off the map

The heart of you makes the sound the vacuum cleaner does when it rolls over a crayon. And then you pour out of your mouth like dirty water, splash and hover just centimeters from the ceiling. You are a swarm of apertures. You are looking in every direction at once, infested with eyes.

You are vibrating with panic, reminded of that time your mother pulled the refrigerator out from the wall to sprinkle the thick green roach-bait powder behind it and thousands of the awful things came streaming out, spreading across the kitchen floor like a flashflood of black desire, purely profane. Your little sister had no hesitation, she ran forward with a warrior-whoop, in just her terry-cloth trainer undies and her cowgirl boots, and began stomping wildly. You stood paralyzed.

You didn't refill the ice cube trays. All three of them are leaning diagonally, in blue plastic repose, in the dish drainer on the left side of the sink downstairs. Your husband Dan complains about that all the time. He'll talk about it you think, in the future, after he discovers your body in its rigorously mortal state, when all the sad-eyed casserole-bearers come parading through, offering condolences with their Frito pies and tuna fish mac-n-cheeses. He'll say *I found all the ice cube trays empty, goddammit, I always hated that* and then he'll sputter like a car with a failing fuel pump.

You look down at him lying there in bed, shirtless in the heat, flat on his back, his chest rising and falling rhythmically. He's snoring, as usual. It's a wonder you could manage dying with all the racket. You think it might be satisfying to see him naked one last time. You will yourself closer, fanning out over his warm skin, but just as you reach out to pull at the elastic waistband of his pajama pants, you realize you have no hands, no arms.

And you are launched as if from a slingshot, backwards, out of the house through the open window, flying involuntarily, rocketed into the firmament, revolving around the earth at unbelievable speed. Starry smears blur by as you hurtle through the universe. You make a complete circuit, slam back into your body and lurch upright, your lungs heaving. You look around you in the dark, your movements jerky like a lizard or a small rodential animal. You scream.

Dan startles awake *What? What? What the fuck?*

I...I forgot to fill the ice cube trays.

Fuuuuck he groans. *Seriously?* And he turns over, falls back asleep facing the wall.

In the morning, walking your son Charlie to school, you have to be deliberate about putting one foot in front of the other. It takes some concentration. It took you a ridiculously long time to make a sandwich to nestle into his TARDIS lunchbox. And when it was finally done, you remembered that peanut butter is an outlaw in elementary school, and had to start all over with bologna and lettuce leaves.

That was pretty dumb of you Charlie said, kicking the trash can with his new sneakers. *Peanuts are a good way to kill somebody, though.*

He's running ahead now, under a milky sky. There's thunder. He turns, smiling, the little pink tip of his tongue like an earthworm poking through the double-gap where his front teeth used to be.

Dragons! he calls back to you, winky-eyed. *They're going to eat you all up!*

He squeals with glee.

Mangle mangle mangle he drones.

When Charlie was littler, you told him that thunder and lightning were dragons. You told him that's why he had to take cover in a storm.

You would be so tasty! A big fat tasty Mama! Crispy!

You look up, not sure what to expect. There could be dragons up there after all.

You deposit him safely at school, and as you walk back toward home, the rain comes down in sheets. You're soaked. You should have brought that thing. That thing, but you can't remember what it's called.

You sit at your kitchen table, your hand clutching a chipped mug of peppermint tea. You have to get your bearings. You have to get a hold on yourself. You haven't yet filled the ice cube trays, but you can't bring yourself to do it.

You had a discussion with Charlie just yesterday about how it isn't appropriate to make fun of people who are sick. There'd been a television program that upset you, his laughter burrowing under your skin like a shovel-faced insect.

Knock knock he'd said.

Who's there? you'd asked.

Leprosy. He'd paused, his grin slimy. *You mean like that?*

You almost wish he were here now, across the table from you, you'd even ask him *Leprosy who?* You don't want to be alone in the house, you could die today alone in the house. You could die today, again.

You call Dan at work, tell him, whispery into the receiver *I died last night.*

Seriously? You called me at work for this? I'm busy. Do you need some attention?

People say that like it's something outrageous. *Doing it for attention.* Like attention is something unnecessary, as if it is a vulgarity.

You may have died just for attention.

Umbrella. Yes, that's it. Umbrella. You take your umbrella and go next door, to Debbie's house. Debbie is a woman, a woman in all the ways you are not. She smells like baby powder, vanilla. She never cuts her own bangs. She carries an endless variety of purses instead of a tote bag. You've always had the suspicion that Debbie would love to tell you just what is wrong with you.

You sit at her kitchen table, a Bloody Mary centered prettily on the daisy-print placemat in front of you. You crunch into the celery stick and droplets of tomato juice speckle the front of your cheap rayon blouse. Debbie hands you a paper napkin, smiles with a little flush of embarrassment for you.

I'm just feeling today like I don't know who I am you say, watching her spread her fingers delicately across the placemat in front of her. She examines her manicure instead of looking at you. *Could you please describe me? I mean, what I'm like, what I've been like before today?*

Her eyebrows lift. She sighs. *Oh, sweetie.*

No, really you say. *Go ahead.*

Well, look she says making eye contact with an earnest pinch of her lips *if you really want to be a better you, there's no better time than right now...*

You nod, solemnly.

You remember when Maddy and Austin were taking care of that frog for their biology unit? They named it after you, sweetie.

So...I'm like...a frog?

Well, I mean, there's nothing so wrong exactly about reptiles, sweetie, the Lord made them, but—

Amphibians.

What? she asks.

A frog is an amphibian.

Yes, well, you wear sweatpants to the grocery store.

Debbie tilts her head to the side, fondles a ringlet of her smooth and shiny hair as you take a gulp of your Bloody Mary. You wipe your upper lip with the crumpled paper napkin. You are an amphibian, in a sweatpantsy way.

Did you want to go ahead and put in a Tupperware order this time around? she asks.

You decide that your project for the day will be to bring down all the boxes of clothes from the attic, reorganize them. Off-season clothes, outgrown clothes; you're sure much of it could be donated to the thrift store. It seems like a nice long project to fill up the afternoon. Repetitive folding is always soothing to you.

You carry each box down the narrow attic stairs, stack them like oversized kids' blocks throughout the living room. A castle in progress, waiting for a giant hand to wreck it. You're sure Charlie would be up for it, if he found a way to swell to monstrous proportions. He'd probably wreck you, too. Crush you under massive sticky thumbs.

There are Spider-Man pajamas in every size, from infant to big boy. Little overalls, little sweaters, little hats and socks and shoes. Dinosaur t-shirts, robot t-shirts, rocketship t-shirts. Hallowe'en costumes. Husband's winter coat, long johns, flannel shirts, that furry hat. Your thick wool poncho, a dozen different scarves in all sizes from the time you took up knitting. Nobody liked the scarves, nobody wore them.

The Hallowe'en costumes. Yes, there it is. The big rubber dragon mask you wore three years ago. Green and purple painted scales, yellow-rimmed eyeholes, a long snout, curling crimson flames shooting from its toothy jaws. It slides over your head easily, smells good inside, in a weird way. Band-Aidy. You sit Indian-style in the middle of your living room rug, unfolding and refolding all the clothes, with a big rubber dragon mask on your head.

The heart of you is not a frog. It is a dragon.

You say it out loud *The heart of me is not a frog. It is a dragon.*

You say it three times.

You stop with the unfolding and refolding, and you sit up straighter, nostrils flaring beneath the mask, as if you smell something in the air.

You walk into the kitchen, with your dragon head on, and carefully fill each little cube-shaped cavity in the blue plastic trays. You place each of the three trays into the freezer compartment, and shut the refrigerator door gently and slowly, as if you tucked them in to bed and don't want them to wake when you sneak out of the room.

You go upstairs and you change out of your jeans and into your favorite sweatpants. They are maroon and wide-legged, without elastic on the ankles. You smash your son's piggy bank on the bathroom tiles and pocket all of his birthday cash. Then you start moving the clothes in great armfuls out onto the front lawn. You get the gas can from the garage, and the wooden matches.

The heart of you makes the sound the vacuum cleaner does when it rolls over a crayon. But you keep driving. You fled the scene of the crime. You think maybe it shouldn't be a crime, burning your own clothes, at your own house, in your own front yard, with your own gasoline, while wearing your own big rubber dragon mask. But here you are, a middle-aged dragon-headed mother in maroon sweatpants and a tomato-juice splattered rayon blouse, swerving and gunning the engine of your blue 2006 Honda Odyssey minivan full of petrified french fries, taco fossils.

The streets are slick from the thunderstorm. The rain has exhausted itself and lies indolent in puddles. It's probably complaining, asking for a blanket or a sandwich, but you speed by, extend one middle finger toward it again and again as it reflects the turnip-colored sky.

Debbie stood watching from her bay windows, her lipsticked mouth forming a perfect zero of shock. Mrs. Kim from across the street bobbed up and down on her lawn, shouting in Korean. You'd like to think she was cheering you on, but it's not likely. Surely, they called the police. Surely, there are surly nurses with straitjackets prepared for your arrival someplace with pale green walls, someplace where they'll want you to watch game shows and ask to use the bathroom. Someplace where your job will be to *just take it easy*, and to lift your tongue to show you aren't a resister.

There's got to be somewhere you can hide out.

You ditch the minivan in a strip mall parking lot, and set off on foot. You're glad you always wear comfortable shoes. Debbie would be screwed.

The roller rink. The giant neon four-wheeled boot blinks like a beacon in the murk of the overcast afternoon air. You spent hours here after school, nearly every day in junior high, circling and circling under the disco ball. In the evenings, you'd tie your skates together by the laces and sling them over your shoulder to wait for your dad to come pick you up in the wood-paneled station wagon. Some nights you'd wait so long that you'd finish your choose-your-own-adventure book twice, three times, by the light of the huge neon skate, and still be waiting. Your ass would go numb sitting on the concrete before he got there, smelling beery-sour, dots of white froth studding the corners of his mouth. He never wore a seatbelt and he'd get angry about you using yours. *What, you think I'm too drunk to drive?*

There are no other skaters in the place now. The kid behind the skate-rental desk has a soul-patch and bloodshot eyes, and his name tag says *Pete*.

What's with the mask? Pete asks with a suspicious squint. *I don't think that's allowed in here.*

Because what, you're a fucking bank? you reply. You notice it's easier to be mouthy when you are hidden under a big rubber dragon head. Also, when you have burned lots of things in your yard and are on the run from the law.

Look, lady, I don't want any trouble.

No you say. *You wouldn't, would you, Pete? You probably don't want to have to call the cops, or your manager, since you reek of weed. How's about we let the nice crazy lady in the dragon head skate for a while, okay? And while you're feeling friendly, you could turn off this crap and play some Bee Gees. I wanna hear some falsetto.*

You realize this is the most you've spoken out loud all day. You hope he caught everything, because the mask probably muffles the sound of your voice.

Pete stares at you for a second, weighing his options.

Do you have a gun?

What, in my sweatpants? No. No, I do not have a gun. I probably should have taken the gun, but I'm not a bad person, so I don't have the gun.

Pete stares again, mouth-breathing, then shrugs his shoulders.

I know how to work the deep-fryer. You want to eat some free jalapeño poppers with me?

Yeah, Pete. That'd be real nice.

You skate in circles, your arms thrown wide. You skate backwards, remembering your zoom around the galaxy. You spin, you dip down and glide in a crouch, you roll on and on and on. You skate to every Bee Gees tune on the playlist, and then you skate to Journey, Blue Öyster Cult, The Ramones, The Pretenders. You skate until you are breathless and then you skate some more.

Pete has locked the doors. He hung a sign, a pink sheet of paper laminated and attached by little hooks to suction cups that kiss fast to the glass. It says in 48-point Comic Sans MS: *"Private Party"!!!!*

You take a break to smoke a fat doobie and gorge yourself on jalapeño poppers and fountain Cokes bigger than your head. It necessitates taking off your big rubber dragon head. Pete nods when he sees your face for the first time, as if it is what he was expecting.

You're totally not deformed or anything. I knew it.

You tell Pete your story, from the swarm of eyes and the ice cube trays right up to the sanctuary promised by the colossal neon roller skate beckoning to you in the grayish gloom.

Wow he says *you've really lost your shit. And that part about the ice cube trays is really kind of weird, don'tcha think? What do you think that's all about?*

Yeah you agree. *It's pretty wild. I haven't thought too much about the ice*

You want to turn on the TV and see if you're on the news? he asks.

Nah I just want to skate some more, if I'm choosing my own adventure.

It's pretty fucking cool that I get to be in your story says Pete.

Yeah, you're an unlikely hero.

Do you think you should give me a blowjob or something?

No, Pete. No, I do not.

>   *Well, you're pretty hot for an older chick, anyway* he mumbles.
>
>   *Thanks, Pete* you say, patting him on the shoulder. *That means a lot to me. I hope if I die again at the end I don't do it here and get you in trouble.*
>
>   *Oh, shit* says Pete. *I didn't think about that.*
>
>   You roll out onto the smooth, waxed wood of the rink and pick up speed, pulling your mask back on. You hitch up your sagging sweatpants, and throw back your dragon head, bellowing at the top of your lungs *Play "Godzilla" again!*
>
>   And Pete does.

It's just shy of midnight when you and Pete leave the roller rink in his 1998 Plymouth Neon Expresso. The dragon head rests on your lap, its yellow-ringed eyes gazing up at you emptily.

>   *You like the spoiler on the back?* he asks. *I thought it was pretty sweet. It has a dual overhead cam. Do you know what that means?*
>
>   You do not. You shake your head.
>
>   *150 horsepower. Fuck yeah* he says. *The passenger door panel was missing when I bought it, but I thought Shit, weight-savings, man. I could race this fucker, you know.*

He drives you past the parking lot where you abandoned the Odyssey, but it's gone. He drives you past your house, not too slow, and you see there's police tape cordoning off the lawn, and the lights are on in every room. You catch a glimpse of Dan, standing in the living room with empty cardboard boxes piled precariously on the couch behind him. He holds a can of cheap beer in one hand, and the cordless phone in the other, pressed to his ear. You almost feel bad for him. He's still wearing his work suit, his tie loosened but hanging in a limp loop around his neck. You know just how his neck smells. You wonder how Charlie got home from school.

>   *Where to now?* Pete asks as he eases to a stop at the sign at the end of your block.

You hold the dragon head in both hands and cradle it to your breast like you once held Charlie, when he was a honey of a baby in soft Spider-Man jammies, before he was a little shit. Before he had peanut-homicide fantasies.

I'm going off the map you murmur.

Some of it, you write with words. Some of it is just pictures, stick figure hieroglyphs, loops and swirls that would be unintelligible to anybody but you. Crooked lines, circles, vaguely Cyrillic scribbles of backward block letters. Some of it is more about the dance you do to write it, the dance of you bending and turning and lunging more than the product of your motions. You drag your driftwood stick across the sand, carving your story out of the damp soft beach. This is the beach where you used to run with your sister, seagull feathers daggered into your twisted salty locks, pretending to be Native princesses. This is the beach where you used to almost-skinny-dip with your high school boyfriend, taking off your underwear, but always keeping your bra on, holding the bottomless two-liter bottle in one hand, a plastic lighter in the other, using the ocean as your own personal gravity bong.

You dig out your story from the very beginning, stretching it down the shore, starting with the very first memory, that afternoon in your cousin's backyard, toddling so fast that your feet left the grass and you flew over the buttercups laughing, your whole body thrumming with joy. You looked back to call to your cousin to join you, but he was gone, your mothers were gone, you were alone and you sank out of the air like a sudden stone, pressed your forehead to the earth and cried. You start from there.

It comes up and out from the heart of you, those first primal swells of ecstasy and anguish expanding to include everything, every moment, every dream. Every kiss, every fist. Every swallow, every breath. Every itch. Every star and eyelash wished upon. Every song sung, every tooth lost and gained, every fear that lurked with dark tendrils whispering, every prayer spun from ache-drunk bruise-blue threads. Every hungry grasp at love, every iron cruelty pressed into the flesh of others.

Every equation solved, every best bloody mouthful.

You write it, draw it, dance it all, an immense and exhaustive map of you, and at the end it is punctuated with one big rubber dragon head laid gently on the sand, blank eyes turned to the burning ball of the rising sun as it bleaches the stars from the sky. The tide is coming in, washing it all away, and you feel your face changing. Your jaw elongating, opening wide and wider. You feel your shoulder blades spreading, wings burgeoning. Your sweatpants are rent to pieces, your stained blouse is wreckage. You are spangled with scales of gleaming purples, iridescent greens. You thunder.

ANNA LEA JANCEWICZ lives in Norfolk, Virginia, where she homeschools her two children, and teaches creative writing and People's History for a homeschool co-op. She is Editor in Chief of *Rabble Lit*, a magazine for working class literature, which promotes anti-racist proletarian solidarity. Her writing has been chosen for The Best Small Fictions, Literary Hub Daily, and the Wigleaf Top 50 longlist, and has appeared at *Hobart*, *Necessary Fiction*, *Pithead Chapel*, and many other venues.